Short Bursts

A Collection of Crime Stories

By

Veronica Moore

To Jackie

Best Wishes
Veronica Moore.

About the Author

Veronica Moore was born and educated in Durban, South Africa. After meeting Ken, she moved to England where they were married in 1972. He was in the Royal Navy. They had several moves before he retired and they settled in Stockport. They have two sons, the eldest is married with two daughters and the younger lives at home.

Until her retirement, Veronica worked in accounts departments in various companies and studied for professional qualifications. Always a voracious reader, Veronica reads anything and everything, her favourite authors being Wilbur Smith and Jilly Cooper. Veronica's writing was initially restricted to communicating with family and friends. She maintains a diary, personal travelogues of her holidays and is researching her family history.

Her other interests are patchwork and quilting, gardening, birdwatching and making greetings cards to send to family and friends. She holds memberships of the Royal Society for the Protection of Birds, the National Trust and the Royal Horticultural Society as well as other organisations.

Acknowledgements

Attending a Creative Writing Course introduced me to Suzanne Downes who was the course tutor. Her enthusiasm and encouragement have been boundless.

Another writer who has given me endless encouragement and advice in the production of this collection is Barbara Fagan Speake who I met through patchworking. After enrolling for Suzanne's course, I discovered that they knew each other and both organised writing groups.

I also want to thank my family for giving me the time and space to indulge in my fantasy, as well as close friends for supporting me in my times of angst when a story wasn't working the way I wanted it to.

I take full responsibility for any errors in these pages.

About this Collection

I felt that it was a pity not to share some of the products of the creative writing course and the writing groups with everyone.

The 99-word stories, introduced to the crime writing group by Barbara Fagan Speake, are fun to write. I have interspersed them amongst longer pieces. The stories were inspired by a photo or a phrase taken randomly from a book. The longer stories started life in a shorter form but my enthusiasm for the subject carried me to greater lengths.

Enjoy the read.

Contents

Double Life

Everything was going well for Simon Cotton. His legitimate business was successful and after this drop today, he would stop dealing with Jack and his illegal business. He had collected the goods from the secure storage and had the list Jack had given him of people waiting for their supplies. At Jack's lock-up, he split the package into the required amounts, wearing gloves and overalls. He was always careful about taking the overalls home to wash afterwards.

When the packages were ready, Simon used his burner phone to let the dealers know he was on his way. There were pre-arranged venues for each one. The cash was concealed in a secret place where Simon then left the drugs. The arrangement meant that he didn't see the dealers, nor they him.

After the exchange, he headed back home, putting the overalls into the washing machine and securing the cash. After a freshen up and change of clothes, he drove his Jaguar to the office. There he found that Jack had left a message. When Simon returned the call, he sensed something was wrong. It was the tone of Jack's voice and the urgent request to meet him at the lock-up, without explaining why.

Simon was mystified but not overly concerned. He left his office, telling his PA that he would see her the next day. He didn't like to take his Jaguar to the lock-up as it was in a rough area, so he retrieved his van, leaving the car safely in his garage.

He arrived at the lock-up half an hour later. There was no sign of Jack's car. Simon felt his heart beating faster. This was strange, very strange. Jack should be there. The padlock was secured. He used his keys to unlock it. He pushed the door gently, not knowing what he would find.

'Bloody hell, Jack … Jack.' His gaze focused on the body hanging from the rafters. The sight was grotesque, eyes wide open, as if in shock and the tongue jutting out.

'Oh my God, Jack, what have you done?' he found himself uttering. He started shaking, holding his head in his hands. What should he do? Touch the body, not touch the body? The stench of faeces was awful.

It took a few minutes to realise there was a note attached to the body: 'I've had enough of this game. Look after Joan for me.'

Simon backed out of the lock-up as quickly as he could. Outside, he leaned against the wall, trying to control his breathing, wanting to throw up. When he felt able to speak again, he dialled 999.

****

He was instructed to wait where he was; an ambulance and the police were on their way. He sent a text to the dealers on the burner phone, using the pre-arranged code in case of any trouble: 'Job Done'.

He reviewed everything in his mind as he waited. The dealers didn't know where the lock-up was. It was in Jack's name, so anything found there would lead back to Jack. There was no CCTV in the vicinity to reveal he had been there in the morning. He finally let out a deep breath: he would be off the police radar.

The sirens alerted him. The ambulance was first, followed almost immediately by the police.

Simon was told to wait while the two police officers went into the lock-up with the paramedics. Then one stayed inside while the other came out to Simon.

'I'm Detective Mark Long. You are?'

'Simon Cotton.'

'When did you discover the body?'

3

'Only ten minutes ago. Jack Ware, that's him, phoned me and asked me to meet him here.'

'Did he say why?'

'No.'

'What time was that?'

'I arrived at my office at eleven-thirty this morning and rang him straight away. It took me over an hour to get home to collect my van because the traffic was heavy. Then another half hour to get here.'

Detective Long considered the timescale and it all seemed accurate.

'How long have you known him?'

'Years, maybe eight or nine. I used to store my second-hand furniture in here but I've now got larger premises so don't need to do that anymore. I've still got a key and that's how I got in. I expected Jack to be here. When his car wasn't outside, I let myself in and found him.'

'Who's Joan?'

'Joan Ware, Jack's wife. I haven't told her yet. I thought of seeing her myself once the ambulance and yourselves had arrived. Would that be alright?'

'I'm afraid, Sir, that's our job. You can come along. We'll follow you to Jack's home. I'll do the talking.'

Simon had no choice, even though it wasn't what he would have liked to happen. They didn't take long to get to the family home. Joan was in and shocked when she saw the officer standing at the door next to Simon.

'What's happened? Why are the police here, Simon?

'There's been an incident, Mrs Ware. Could we come in?' The detective didn't give Simon a chance to say anything.

'Yes, by all means, come into the living room. Sit down anywhere.' Joan was unnerved and sent a questioning look to Simon. After introductions, the detective told her what they had found.

'No, no it can't be.' She covered her face, not believing what the detective was saying. Simon went to the kitchen for a glass of water for her.

'Did you have any idea your husband was on the verge of suicide or harming himself?'

'No, not at all. His business is flourishing. I don't have any idea why he would take his own life.'

'What business is he involved in, then?'

'The sale of furniture, which also requires some importation of items. Surely you would've seen crates at the warehouse? He said he'd received a delivery earlier this week.'

'He wasn't found at his warehouse. He was found at a lock-up on Sandy Lane.'

'I thought he got rid of that place ages ago, when Simon no longer needed it for storage.' She looked across at Simon, who said nothing but shrugged his shoulders.

'Where is the warehouse? Who has keys for it? Will anyone be there now?' The detective was firing questions at her and Joan was getting upset.

'The warehouse is on the Greenfield Industrial Estate. There are spare keys here. He has two storemen working for him, Tim Brown and Peter Frith.'

'We'd like to take those keys, Mrs Ware.'

Joan stood up and went to the kitchen drawer. There was a shuffling and then the sound of the drawer slamming shut.

'Jack must have taken them. There must be someone else at the warehouse with his keys.'

'I'll look into this myself now. I'll probably need to see you again to ask you more questions. Can I have both of your contact details?'

Simon handed him his business card with all his details and also gave him his home address. Joan gave him her home and mobile telephone numbers.

'Would Mr Ware have driven himself to the lock-up?'

'I assumed so, Detective.' Simon didn't know for sure how Jack had arrived there, nor did Joan.

'I'll check with his staff.'

Once Detective Long had left, Simon hugged Joan, who burst into tears.

'I'm sorry this has happened, Joan. I don't know what could've made him do this. Maybe something will come out of the police enquiries.'

'Do you think he knew about us? He's always seemed too busy to see what was going on under his nose.'

'I'd spoken to him yesterday and he seemed fine. It must be something that happened today that tipped him over the edge. His car wasn't at the lock-up either.'

'How did he get there then? There's more to this. Maybe someone else did it and made it look like a suicide.'

'We'll leave it to the police to find that out.'

The only thing bothering Simon was how to get rid of that burner phone.

****

Detective Long's arrival at the warehouse caused some concern for the two storemen.

After he introduced himself and ascertained who they were, he questioned the two men.

'What time did Mr Ware leave these premises today?'

'He was only in first thing for a short while, then said he was going to his office in the
showroom. Why are you asking?' Tim couldn't understand why the police were there at all.

'Can you vouch for that, Mr Frith?'

'Call me Peter. What Tim has told you is true. He left before we had our morning coffee break. Is that relevant? Where is he?'

'What do you know of Simon Cotton?'

'He's friends with Jack - Mr Ware and his wife Joan. Mind, more with Joan than the boss, if you ask me. He comes around here from time to time. Used to work here but started his own second-hand furniture business. Generally, Jack sells him furniture he has taken in part exchange for new stuff from some customers.' Peter was getting into his stride.

'They've been business associates for years and friends. Both their businesses seem to be doing well. We send a lot of stuff Simon's way and when his customers want something special, Jack can usually help. What's this all about, Officer?'

Tim was feeling uneasy. He knew about the packages that came in with some of the furniture. Jack said they contained extra fittings in case they were needed but they weren't heavy enough for that. Also, they were securely sealed with no labelling. He was always told to put them in the locked hatch at the back of the warehouse. It had strong locks on it and could be opened from the outside. He wasn't aware if Peter knew anything about the hatch. It had never been discussed.

'Mr Ware was found dead in his lock-up this morning by Mr Cotton.'

'Never. Heart attack?' Peter was straight in there with questions.

'No, he was found hanging.' He was watching Tim's reaction as he had been quiet.

'Why? Why did he do it?' Tim at last found his voice. He couldn't believe that Jack would do that to himself.

'We're not sure if he did commit suicide, actually. The forensics team are working in the lock-up at the moment. They'll draw conclusions from anything they find. We wondered if his staff knew anything about it. By the way, what car was he driving when he left here?'

'It'll be his grey Mercedcs. He loves that car and cares for it well. Purrs along when he leaves here.' Peter spoke with envy.

'Do you know the registration number?'

'JW 75. It's his birth year and initials. A bit of a show-off. Joan gave the plate to him for his fortieth birthday a few years back.'

'Where is the main showroom situated? Who else works for him?'

'There's his secretary, Valerie. She never comes here, just stays at the office in the showroom. That's at the back of the Orange Centre down the road. Also, two salesmen work there. They sometimes come here to look at the new stuff coming in. Helps them with the sales, they say. I think it's to get out of the store when they're bored. Then two drivers/delivery men. We've one truck which is used to transport the furniture where it needs to go.' Tim was willing to talk now.

'I or some of my colleagues may need to speak to you again. Can you give me your personal details so we know where to contact you at any time?' The detective added that information to the notes he had made of what they had said. Formal statements would have to follow later.

Once Detective Long had left, they looked at each other. Peter was first to speak.

'I wonder what that's all about? Do you think he did it? Can't see that happening really. Would love to go and have a look.'

'You always look at the gory side of life, don't you Peter? I'm more concerned about where we go from here? What's going to happen to our jobs? If he didn't do it, who did and why? Too many questions. I think we should tidy up in here and go to the showroom. See if we can find anything out from Valerie. She'll be in shock.'

The two men finished off their work, locked up and headed for the showroom. It was nearly home time but they wanted to find out more if they could.

****

George, one of the salesmen, showed Detective Long into Valerie's office. He would've liked to stay around but there were customers who needed his attention.

'Good afternoon, Detective. I'm Valerie James, secretary to Jack Ware.'

'Afternoon, Mrs James. I'm Detective Long. I've some bad news concerning your boss. Jack Ware was found dead at his lock-up this afternoon by Mr Simon Cotton.' He paused as she looked ready to faint.

'No. I don't believe it. You can't be right. There must be something wrong. Are you sure? I need to sit down.'

'This must come as a shock to you. Can I get you a drink of something?'

'I have water. Oh, dear. Does Mrs Ware know?'

'Yes, I've just come from there. Mr Cotton is with her. He called us in. He was to meet Mr Ware. Did you know anything about that?' Valerie didn't and told him so. She was shaking.

'Can you tell me what time he left here?'

'Yes, it was just after lunch. He wasn't in a good mood. He had a visitor this morning about eleven, a big burly chap. He was very aggressive. I couldn't hear exactly what was said but it was about some faulty delivery. After he had gone, I asked Jack which delivery it was. He said to mind my own business and get back to my office. He was on the phone for a while then rushed out, slamming his door behind him. I've never seen him behave like that.'

'Did he drive himself?'

'Yes. Where is his car?'

'Would that be the grey Mercedes that he drove from the warehouse this morning? The storemen told me the make and registration number.'

'Yes. Is it at the lock-up if he was found there?'

'No, it isn't there. I'll put a call out for it. It may have been stolen.'

'This gets worse by the minute.' Valerie was shaking her head.

'Is that his office?' He nodded to the clear window between Valerie and Jack's offices.

'Yes, it is.'

'A set of keys to the warehouse is missing. Are they here?'

'Which set is that?'

'Mrs Ware said there was a spare set at her house but couldn't find them. She thought Mr Ware must have brought them here.'

'I didn't know about them. I'll have a look in his office.'

'Don't touch anything until the forensics team have been in. Expect them tomorrow. I'll just have a quick look around.'

Valerie opened the interconnecting door to let the detective through. He spent several minutes in there and then returned to her office.

'Hypothetically, can you think of any reason why Mr Ware would kill himself or be a homicide victim?'

'No. As far as I'm aware the business is doing well. He and his wife seem happy, not that I mix with them socially. The accountant, Mr Morley, doesn't seem overly concerned about the business.' She tried to think straight about all aspects of the business but all sorts of thoughts were buzzing about in her head.

'Well, I'll leave you for now and try to trace that car of his. We might find something out from that.'

'Goodbye, Detective. Will you keep us informed?'

'As much as we can. It may be some time before we have any answers.'

The detective had only been gone a few minutes when the two storemen arrived. Valerie told them to wait in her office. When she returned, she had a tray with mugs of coffee and biscuits.

'I think we could all do with a hot drink while we chat. What a shock. Do either of you know what this could be about? I can't believe it.' The two men took their coffees and a couple of biscuits each. They were deep in thought and no wiser than Valerie appeared to be. It would take them some time to process what this would mean to them.

'Valerie, do you think he actually did it to himself?'

'Until today, like I've said to the detective, I wouldn't have thought Jack had any problems. Did he go to the warehouse?'

'Yes, that was first thing this morning,' Peter answered. 'He looked around the back of the warehouse and we heard him slamming doors. We kept out of his way, thinking it was just a bad day. Wonder what it's all about?'

'I'm more concerned about what happens with our jobs. Will the firm keep going, do you think? Can Joan run it?' Tim was more practical and worried about his finances. With a family and mortgage, things were different for him. Peter lived with his girlfriend who already had a house, so didn't have the same financial worries.

'Joan hasn't been in touch yet. I'll contact her tomorrow. I think we just carry on and keep our customers happy. We'll do a stock check tomorrow morning. If you two can see to that at the warehouse, I'll ask George and Alan to do one here. We have a few orders outstanding for delivery, so we can get those sorted out. I'll get in touch with the accountant and make sure I'm doing the right thing. He'll have to consult with Joan. We do seem to be doing well and she'll need an income. Hopefully she'll take over.'

'Thanks, Valerie. That's a weight off for now. Can you keep us informed? The uncertainty will be awful.' Tim felt a little easier but wasn't happy about Jack's death.

'Hopefully you can have a good night's rest before the stock take tomorrow. If you need help from the drivers, Bill and Clive, let me know in the morning. Have you got your keys to the warehouse and is everything safe and locked up there, Tim?'

'You don't really need to ask that, do you Valerie? We value our jobs.' This time Peter was more serious. Suddenly he realised that things could turn sour for all of them.

They said their goodbyes and the men left. Valerie called the salesmen in once the customers had left and the doors were locked. She updated them with the news. They were both shocked.

'What now? Where do we go from here?' Alan was the first to speak.

'We carry on as before. We come in tomorrow and do the stock take. I'll phone Christopher Morley, the accountant. He'll most probably come to see us but will need to speak to Joan as well. She'll be under a terrible strain. I believe Simon Cotton is with her.' A smirk passed between the two men.

'I don't believe Simon has anything to do with this at all. Home time, I think. We have a busy day tomorrow.'

While the two salesmen left, talking softly to themselves, Valerie tidied up her office then looked across to Jack's. The detective had looked over his desk, touching nothing, so everything was as Jack had left it. The investigating team would come and have a look at what was currently on the desk. He had also asked how many phones Jack had. She had told him that he had one for business and one for personal use, as far as she knew. Sometimes she did wonder, though, as he would pull one out of his pocket when the others were on his desk. She pushed that knowledge to one side.

Valerie didn't know what to think or do. She was not used to leaving the office without a last word with Jack. The temptation to look through his desk was strong but she knew she had to leave it all alone. And she was mystified as to the unknown visitor's identity. How did Jack know such a character? She decided to phone the accountant.

'Christopher, a terrible thing has happened. Jack has been found dead, hanged.' Valerie couldn't keep the panic out of her voice and just blurted this over the phone before even greeting the accountant.

'Valerie, hello. What are you saying?'

'The police have been. Jack was in his lock-up and found by Simon Cotton. It's all been horrible. I tried to be calm with the staff here and said we would do a stock take in the morning. I don't even know why I said that. It just seems the right thing to do.'

'Valerie, I have a busy night at home with the family tonight. I'll call round first thing in the morning and chat with you. But I will contact Joan tonight. How is she?'

'I don't know. The police said Simon was with her but I don't know if he's still there. She does have a sister and mother in the area. Do you think I should phone her?'

'I'll sort that out. Are you on your own there? Can you lock up and leave securely?' She saw the salesmen putting their jackets on and walking towards her office.

'George and Alan are coming to say goodnight. I'll ask them to stay while I lock up the offices so we can leave together.'

'Good. I'll see you in the morning. Make sure you get home safely.'

'I will. See you tomorrow.'

She shivered with the thought that someone may be lurking outside. There were plenty of security lights but also dark corners.

'Just coming to say goodnight. Are you going home now, Valerie? We'll help you lock up. Strange without the boss here.' George was trying to be solicitous but would love to know more.

'Yes, I'm going home and it is strange. Have you checked all the doors and side entrances?'

'Yes, we did all that. Just the alarm to set now when you've finished.' Alan was the more serious and reliable of the two. George was the better salesman.

'Won't be a mo. I'll meet you at the door.' Valerie checked her cabinets and drawers then went into Jack's office to do the same there. She used her keys to lock his drawers and the filing cabinet which he hadn't done, unusually, before leaving his office. Shivers kept running down her spine.

She duly locked both doors and left the security light on. The men were waiting at the door for her. She watched as they set the alarm then they all stepped outside. They made sure she was safely in her vehicle.

'We'll see you in the morning, Val. Try to relax tonight.'

'Thank you, both of you. Have a good night yourselves. Maybe we'll learn a bit more tomorrow.'

****

Simon had left Joan's house to attend to his business. He was feeling upset with the sight that had met him at the lock-up. He had managed to keep his cool but now he could reflect on the day's events. He took the van home and got his car out, almost robotically. Driving to his showroom, he mulled the problem over.

He wondered if there was a problem with the supply of the drugs. Everything had seemed correct. The weights were not altered. He didn't take drugs himself, so was not aware of what a bad batch would look or taste like. His burner phone was quiet. He had misgivings about one delivery where the person was already there and waiting, when usually he didn't see the person. The man knew the password, the venue was correct and the money was also correct, so Simon had completed the exchange. He was glad it would be his last deal with Jack in this respect. He was now left with the money. No way of handing that over to Jack. He knew Jack paid up as soon as the delivery came in, so the supplier wouldn't be chasing Jack for money.

No, there was no reason to believe it was to do with the drugs. It could only be the furniture business. But why meet at the lock-up? Where was Jack's car? And now the police were combing that lock-up. He tried to think of when he had put on the gloves and taken them off. The equipment was in a cupboard and that would be found. His finger marks would be found there as he had used that lock-up legitimately. He would have to wait and see what else the police found.

In his office, after he had attended to his affairs, he decided to telephone Valerie. He knew she would've left work but had her mobile number in case of emergencies.

'Hi Valerie. How are you? An awful shock today.'

'Oh, Simon, it's so horrible. How are you after finding Jack like that?'

'I'm a bit numb, Valerie. I can't understand why Jack would do this. Have you any ideas?'

'No. My head is aching with the questions in it. How's Joan? Did you stay with her for long? Is she on her own?'

'I left her late in the afternoon as I had my business to see to. She phoned her sister and mother. They were going to see her. I think the police are going to speak to her again. They may leave that until they have done some preliminary investigations. She was upset about it and shocked.'

'I wonder what it's all about. And his car is missing. Who could have taken that?'

'That's a mystery. If someone arranged to meet Jack there, they must have had transport to get there. Why pinch Jack's car? It's too conspicuous to just cruise around in and not get caught.'

'Simon, do you know any of Jack's acquaintances who is big, dark hair combed back from his face? Mean eyes. Big chin. Really rough looking? He came to see Jack just before Jack left the office in a temper. The man was shouting at Jack about a faulty delivery or something. I couldn't quite hear all of it through the doors. Jack was really angry. Before he left, I asked him what delivery it was and he almost bit my head off, telling me to mind my own business.'

'What time was that? I had a call from him to meet me at the warehouse. That was around lunchtime.'

'It was around that time. I don't know, Simon, there are too many questions buzzing around in my head. I wonder if we'll ever know the truth of it all.'

Simon was quiet for a moment, considering what Joan had revealed. She ended the silence.

'Is your business still doing well? We may have some pieces coming in, you know, part exchange for new goods. I'm in touch with the accountant. He's coming to see me tomorrow but is contacting Joan as well. I don't know if she'll be in a fit state to think about the business.'

'Yes, everything is rather up in the air now for all of you at the shop. I can only say, work with the accountant. Christopher Morley, isn't it? Maybe Joan will feel up to taking an active interest in it now. Are you due any more shipments from abroad?'

'There is a crate due in from Thailand in fourteen days. The last crate that came in a couple of days ago was from China. No more orders have been placed with that company. I think that Jack was not pleased with the quality of the furniture coming from there. That's the problem when its mass produced – low standards creep in.'

'Maybe that's so. Some of the pieces I sell, although second-hand, are much better than some of the stock Jack's been receiving. Well, if I can do anything for you, Valerie, any way I can help at all, just give me a call.'

'I will, Simon. Thank you very much for your concern. It's a terrible shock.'

'Try to relax and make sure you eat and sleep. Bye for now.'

'Bye, Simon and thanks once again.'

****

Simon was thoughtful as he ended the call. Jack hadn't mentioned knocking the other trade on the head. Who was the man who visited him before he rushed out? Was the visit anything to do with his demise?

He reflected on the past nine years.

Simon had moved to the area when his marriage broke down and he wanted a fresh start. He had been in sales all his life and quite successful. As he was continually away from home, his wife had socialised a lot with her friends and met someone else. They didn't have any children, so there was nothing keeping them together. Simon hadn't had time to form any relationships himself, concentrating on making a new life for himself with his business.

He had answered an advert for an instore salesman that Jack had placed. Jack was impressed with his experience and employed him as a manager in his new showroom. It wasn't long before they both realised that Simon wanted more than working for someone, so Jack helped finance him to set up on his own. The second-hand business was beneficial to both of them.

Simon didn't know about Jack's illegal activities until Jack was let down by his delivery driver. He desperately needed someone to distribute the drugs when they came in and approached Simon. Simon was reluctant to get involved but Jack convinced him by reducing his debt. That was a hard offer to turn down. Simon made it clear that it would only be for as long as the debt was repaid. He was against the whole concept of the drug trade and hated himself for getting caught up in it. Apart from that, he and Jack got on very well.

There was an immediate attraction between him and Joan when they met. Simon kept her at arm's length initially. It was only over the past two years that they had become intimate but only occasionally, as they both had a lot of respect for Jack. Simon understood that Joan knew nothing of Jack's illegal activities.

As it was getting late, Simon decided to head for home. His staff had left soon after he arrived as there were no customers about. Driving home, he thought about his activities and if the police would rumble him. He had already arranged for his van to have a service and the lining refurbished as it was worn. The woollen lining protected the furniture in transit. He would wash the wool rugs which were used to separate and protect items.

Tossing and turning in bed, Simon couldn't sleep. He decided to get up and have a hot drink. While sitting in the quiet of the night, still thinking about the day, he recalled his last drop off. Something bothered him about that. He decided to wait till morning, then contact the chap.

As he had not spoken to the contacts, just communicated by text messaging, he did the same again.

'Hi John. Was everything ok with the delivery yesterday?'

It wasn't long before there was a reply.

'Can I phone you?'

Simon decided to telephone John instead. What he found out in a way shocked him but it satisfied his concerns.

'What's the problem, John?'

'I've been in hospital. I had a run-in with a guy who was trying to muscle in on my dealing. He wanted my supply. He attacked me and if I hadn't told him how I got the stuff, he would've killed me. He may as well have done it anyway. My main man didn't get his share and is after me. He is going ape and his heavies are causing mayhem.'

'How badly are you injured?'

'Broken nose, puffed eye but can still see, cut on my jaw which is stitched, broken arm, three cracked ribs and sprained ankle where they stood on it and twisted it. They kept me in for two nights on observation but no internal injuries. Lucky me.'

'What do these men look like? The guy who knocked you about? And the person you call the main man?'

'The bully boy is Lucas. Tall, fair hair and a pockmarked face. Thin. Wears tracksuit bottoms all the time and a black jumper.'

Standard gear for the dealers, Simon thought. The description also fitted the chap who took the delivery yesterday.

'The main man is large, burly, mean face and eyes, big chin. I wouldn't mess with him if I could help it.'

'What is the main man's name? Does he know where you live? Are you safe? What do you intend doing?' Simon was concerned for the chap's welfare even though he didn't need to be. People choose their own path in life, mostly, although some go astray because of necessity.

'I shouldn't tell you but he is Deon Massey. Horrible man, stay away from him. They don't know my pad. I'm giving this life up, anyway. I left home in the Midlands to make a go up north but think I'll go back to me Mum. She'll be pleased. She worries. Probably end up working in a supermarket for the rest of me life. Better than being knocked about by rubbish.'

'Will these other people be able to trace you?

'Not if I can help it. Going to change my phone and get rid of everything to do with this side of things. Not having any coppers tracing me. Think between the two, there's gonna be a war.'

'Well, get yourself out of the Manchester area ASAP. Are you ok for money for now?'

'Yeh, got a secret stash. Going to get going today. Packed last night.'

'Good for you. Be careful and good luck.'

'Thanks. Don't know your name but watch your back. Something funny going on round here.'

'Cheers John. I'll be careful. One last thing, get rid of all our messages and this number. Ok?'

'Sure will. Don't want anyone tracing me, ever.'

Simon hoped he would. Well, a lot of revelations in that short chat. As he would not be using that phone or number again, he downloaded all the info from the phone onto the SIM. He took it out of the phone and placed the phone in a strong plastic bag. In his garage, he smashed the phone. Could be traces of powder on it. He put the SIM in a tin, poured a little paraffin on it and set it alight. It flared up but caused no damage to anything else. In the end there was only a charred-up piece of metal left. Once it cooled, he wrapped that in paper towel he kept in the garage. He took the plastic bag and towel back into the house. He had a meeting in Leeds later, so would dispose of them somewhere on route. Pity he couldn't burn it all.

He hadn't mentioned anything about Jack's death to John as he probably wouldn't have known him. However, John was correct in his feelings that something wasn't right. The only thing bothering Simon was that the thug, Lucas, had seen him, so knew his face. Well, he would just have to trust to some sort of luck that they would never see each other again.

Simon managed to dispose of the paper towel in a bin in the car park at one service area. At another, he dumped the plastic bag in a bin in the bathroom. Hopefully they would never re-surface to haunt him.

****

A week later, two police officers arrived at Simon's showroom to take a statement from him. PC Denise Wainwright and PS Ian Reid had made the appointment, saying it wasn't necessary for him to attend the police station. They had all the paperwork sorted out in no time at all.

'Is there anything else you can add to this statement? Anything that may have some relevance to this case?' PC Wainwright asked the question casually but Simon felt she knew something he didn't.

'No, not that I can think of. I've given you all the information I have about the day and my association with Jack.'

'Well, if you think of anything else, please contact us. We'll be in touch if we need clarification on any points.' The PC gave Simon her card and the two officers left.

That evening, he and Joan met for dinner. They hadn't been meeting often. They didn't want to throw undue suspicion on themselves regarding Jack's death. Neither of them was involved and in that respect they were innocent. Simon told Joan of the interview with the police.

'I had to give my statement two days ago. They came to the house as well. Detective Long was with PC Wainwright. He asked the questions; she took the notes. She has a lovely neat handwriting.'

Women notice the oddest things, Simon mused.

'Did they give you any indication of how their investigation is going?'

'You know they found his car in a supermarket car park in Harrogate? Why there is anyone's guess. They have it for forensic examination. I don't want it back anyway. I'll let the garage take it when they've finished and sell it. I don't know who will have been in it and my Audi is great for me. By the way, I have been into the office with Christopher. He and Valerie are going to show me the ropes and I feel quite excited about getting involved in the business. It will make life more interesting for me. I certainly won't have time to be bored.'

'That may change things between you and me then? Can't mix business with pleasure?' Simon hoped that they could make a life for themselves but it was best to tread carefully until the murder enquiry was settled. That is the way the police were treating the case at the moment.

'We'll have to see.' Joan smiled slightly.

'Valerie said the police had taken away lots of paperwork. She took photocopies of everything in case the information was needed by them in the showroom or Christopher. She is a gem, you know. Jack was lucky to have her. And she knows the business inside out. She could manage it but I'd like to have a go.'

'I think it'll be great for you for many reasons. Not least of all, give yourself more confidence and a different social standing, if that's what you want.'

'Not necessarily that but to feel that my life is more useful in a way. That I'm not just a showpiece but have a brain.'

'Oh, you certainly have that.' They moved on to various subjects and enjoyed the rest of the evening.

****

The following week, Simon was surprised to see police officers walking around his van when it was parked outside his showroom. He went outside to ask if he could help them, then recognised PC Wainwright and PS Reid.

'Hi. Good morning. How can I help you?'

'Is this the van you usually use when you go to Jack Ware's lock-up?'

'Yes but I don't go there much nowadays. Why are you asking?'

'We have a witness who says you were in the vicinity during the morning of the day Mr Ware was found dead.'

'Are you sure? I only went to the warehouse after Jack phoned me that day.'

Simon's heart was beating. He had done his work in the dark, before people were about and the lock-up is in a remote area. He had to bluff this out.

'The registration is the same as that given to us.'

'Isn't there any CCTV that can verify that I wasn't there?'

'No, unfortunately not. So, it's your word against that of our witness.'

'Why would someone say that when it's not true?'

'Have you no idea? You see, we found traces of drugs in that lock-up. Did you have anything to do with that?'

'I don't know anything about that. I don't take drugs. I am not aware that Jack had anything to do with drugs.'

'We would like to take your van away for forensic examination. If it's clean, there's no problem. We can call for the recovery vehicle now, if that's alright?'

'No problem. I was using it today to deliver furniture to a customer but that job's done now. How long will you need it for? I'll have to hire one for any deliveries I'll have to make.'

'As long as it takes to do a thorough check. Maybe a week.'

'Ok, I can let the hire company know how long I'll need a van for.'

He went into the showroom to get his van keys to give to the officers. Kath, his assistant, was amazed at the police wanting to take the van.

'What are you going to do? Why would they want it?'

'A case of mistaken identity, I think. No bother, I'll hire a van for our deliveries. I'll need a lift home to pick my car up. Rick can take me in his banger while you hold the fort.'

As soon as the officers left, he and Rick went to fetch his car. Rick was intrigued and didn't stop asking questions.

'Why do they want it? Who said you were there? What are they going to find?'

'Don't know, don't know and nothing.' Simon was not in the mood for interrogation from anyone, let alone a warehouseman.

34

The van had been thoroughly cleaned, even the front and cubby hole. It had fresh lining and carpets and was in pristine condition. The police may wonder why it had been cleaned so thoroughly recently but he could verify that it had been booked in some weeks before. The job was best done over a weekend. The police had not mentioned finding the drug weighing equipment. Simon wondered if it had been stolen. He had to be on his guard about that.

The niggle started again. That Lucas person. He was involved here somewhere. He was the only one who could connect Simon to the drug dealing. Simon was not going to do anything, just sit it out and see what happened. If Lucas had been rumbled and was trying to wriggle out of something, Simon was not going to help him out and leave himself open to accusations, even though some of it was true.

His van was ready for him to collect after a week. Simon had been on tenterhooks. He asked if everything was ok and was told that PC Wainwright would be in touch if she needed to discuss anything with him. When he arrived at the showroom, she was waiting for him.

'Just one thing to clarify, Mr Cotton. We noticed that your van is newly fitted out with carpets and lining. Any reason for that?'

'I booked it in a couple of months ago. The lining protects the furniture in transit. It was getting shabby and one area was badly torn when a heavy item had caught on it. I had the carpets done at the same time, just to smarten everything up. I have to book it in for any repairs or maintenance well in advance over weekends, when I don't do deliveries very often. I have all the paperwork for that in the office, if you'd like to see it.'

PC Wainwright looked through all the paperwork, taking photos of it on her phone and duly left. She was not leaving anything to chance.

Simon breathed a sigh of relief.

****

The investigation into Jack's death took some months. Joan began to settle into learning the business and enjoyed this new way of life. She and Simon occasionally met for meals and discussed business on a different footing.

The inquest was held and a death from asphyxiation via hanging was considered. The autopsy revealed that the nylon rope used with a slip knot would have caused

Jack to stop breathing within two minutes. Within a further four minutes he would have died due to lack of oxygen reaching his brain. There was evidence from bruising on his body that Jack had also been severely assaulted prior to being hanged. The table in the lock-up had evidence of shoe prints on it. More than one person was responsible for Jack's death.

Simon had to give evidence at that hearing. The timings of the phone call to Simon, Jack leaving the office and Simon arriving at the lock-up were crucial for the police investigation into what was now confirmed as a murder. The perpetrators must have been waiting for Jack at the lock-up.

The police eventually made an appointment to see Joan. They brought her up to date with their progress. They had found out that Jack was involved with the drug trade. They asked her if she was aware of that. She kept quiet, thinking about what had been discovered.

'Mrs Ware, I repeat, did you know about that?'

'No, I didn't know.'

'Have you found the missing keys to the warehouse?'

'No, I don't know where they can be.'

'One of the people who is of interest to us in this investigation is Deon Massey. Do you know him?'

She looked at the photo they showed her and convincingly said she didn't.

'There are others involved in this as well. We shall visit you again when we have more information.' At that point no other names were given.

****

A few days before the trial of Deon Massey was due to start, Simon received a phone call from Joan's solicitor, Malcolm White.

'Joan has been arrested. She is being accused of being the instigator of the death of Jack.'

'What? I can't believe that. If that's true, she's one very good actress. How has this happened?'

'I hope you will treat what I am going to say in full confidence. Joan found out about Jack's drug trade and was horrified and furious. She didn't want anything to do with it and wanted him out of the house. That was around two weeks before his death. She evidently was more than friendly with the salesman, George. She asked him if he knew anyone who could stop Jack's trade. George made enquiries through a chap named Lucas who he knew from his childhood days, growing up in the same neighbourhood. That way, he put Joan in touch with Deon.'

'This is incredible.' Simon felt he had been made a fool of and wondered why the solicitor was telling him all this.

'George had been around at the warehouse on several occasions when the crates arrived from China and had seen what was delivered. He had been as curious as Tim Brown but took it one step further. He had noted how often and that at some point, the storage had emptied. He told Joan this. None of them know who was taking the packages and how. Joan had given the spare warehouse keys to George but had forgotten when the police called on her. I shall be defending Joan in court. She would like you to be there.'

'To tell the truth, Malcolm, I am sickened by all these revelations. I would not have thought Joan would do this to Jack. The police will be closing the business, won't they?'

'Joan is hoping, if she goes to jail as is more than likely, that you will run it with Valerie for her.'

'I shall have to give serious consideration to that before discussing it with Valerie. What happens about George? What is the probable outcome for him?'

'It depends on his history and how the judge views his involvement.'

Simon told Malcolm he would be in touch with him regarding the business proposal. He doubted that he would attend any of the hearings in court. He was not going to risk coming face to face with Lucas in court.

During the conversation with Malcolm, Simon realised that he still had the key to the warehouse storage box on his keyring. He decided to go for a walk to the nearby reservoir that evening. In a secluded area, having checked that no-one else was about, he flung it far into the water. Hopefully it would settle down in the mud and never be found.

He decided that he would not look after Jack's business for Joan. He let Malcolm know the following day. If Jack's business was going to wrap up, he could upgrade his business to new as well as used furniture. There could be an expansion and then take on some of Jack's staff. That was a plan for the future.

****

Simon followed the newspaper reports of the trial closely.

Lucas Childs had followed the activity at the lock-up from a distance, after he'd followed Deon Massey. He'd been intrigued by the enquiries George had made. He wanted to know what was going on, so decided to follow Massey as much as possible. Massey and two accomplices had arrived at the lock-up soon after Jack Ware. Lucas had parked his car behind another derelict building opposite so he could keep an eye on the entrance. He didn't go up to the building as he didn't want to be seen. After about fifteen minutes, the two men came out with some machinery and put it in the boot of Massey's car. Massey locked the padlock on the lock-up, then they drove off.

Lucas wondered what was happening to Jack Ware. He sauntered across and noticed that Jack's keys were still in his car. He decided he would take the Mercedes for a joy ride to Harrogate where he was setting up a new drug deal. He enjoyed the smooth ride, noticing how low the fuel was on the outskirts of Harrogate. He parked the car in a supermarket car park, used public transport to get to his meeting and caught a train back to Manchester, as he had before when not trusting his car to do the journey. CCTV picked him up at the supermarket and his finger marks were all over the car. He was known to the police. When he was accused of murdering Jack, he told the police everything he knew. He went to jail for stealing Jack's car and was facing a further trial for his drug dealing activities.

Joan was sentenced to twelve years for her part in Jack's death. It was likely she would only serve half of that sentence. Deon Massey received the longest sentence for manslaughter. His two henchmen also received similar sentences. All three were facing another trial for their drug dealing activities.

Simon finally felt he could relax and concentrate fully on his business which was legitimate and beginning to expand successfully.

Another Attempt

He heard the loud thump as she fell. He ran up the stairs.

The bathroom door was shut. Barging in, he found her slumped on the floor, unconscious. He phoned for an ambulance, not knowing what else to do. Returning to the bathroom, he touched her face, still warm but deathly white. He covered her with a towel, not daring to move her. The paramedic arrived, examined her and phoned for an ambulance.

'She's not dead but not far off. You say you didn't see what happened?'

The man shook his head. The oily soap hadn't worked this time.

Caught Out

'Don't bother taking your coat off.'

She was so tired and couldn't be bothered to argue.

'Why, where are we going?'

'To your mother's where you're staying tonight.'

'You've arranged this with her? How dare you?'

'The card school is coming here tonight and I want you out. You're going.'

She lunged for him but he was quicker than her. She reeled from the punch and fell to the floor, her head hitting the corner of the skirting with an ear-splitting crack.

Turning round, he saw Mrs Jones from next door standing in the open doorway, iPhone in hand.

Weekend Trickery

She couldn't believe, at first, that he would organise a weekend break for her.

Tracey needed a rest from the daily routine but wished it could include him. Steve had been working long hours. He wanted to tidy the garden over the long weekend. The children, Peter and Charlie, were staying with her sister, Joan and her family.

She was at long last visiting Paris on a coach tour. After Steve had dropped her off at the pick-up point, she didn't have long to wait, along with three couples. Once all the luggage was stowed and they were in their allocated seats, they set off. Tracey soon settled into her seat, luckily next to a window. Travel via the motorway network and the Eurotunnel was smooth. Entering France and travelling through unfamiliar countryside was exciting. They stopped for lunch at a motorway services then carried on to Paris where they had a tour of one part of the city before going to their hotel.

On the second day, while the group were in a church, they could smell smoke. Alarms sounded and they were herded out of the building. Some people were in the basement looking at artefacts. They were trapped. Firefighters didn't manage to get them out.

As she walked swiftly away from the building to seek safety, Tracey was shocked to catch a glimpse of Steve with Sally from the office he worked in. They were standing to one side but hadn't seen her. Her instinct told her not to let him see her. Mingling with a group, she made her way to a park across the road, standing beside a tree from where she could spy on the couple.

She noticed the tour guide come out of the building. He started to gather their party together. Steve and Sally stood nearby. Tracey kept her distance. She began to feel sick. She realised she had her phone in her hand. She took photos of the scene, particularly Steve and Sally. Wanting to let the tour guide know she was safe but not exactly where she was, she phoned him.

'Hi Jerry. Tracey Strong here. Don't look around for me. I'm safe. There's someone in the crowd who I don't want to see. He may approach you to ask about me. Please don't let him know anything about me. Act as if I've disappeared. I'll be back at the hotel when you arrive back there later on. Please do as I ask.'

'Ok, so long as you're alright.'

'I am. I'll explain later.'

She watched as the guide looked around, shook his head and continued to tick people off his list. She hoped he didn't tick her name off in case Steve insisted on looking at the list. Steve made no attempt to approach the firefighters who had sealed off the entrance with tape, nor the policemen standing guard. She saw him walk over to the tour guide and speak to him. The guide shook his head and shrugged his shoulders. He would have to report the names of missing people to the authorities.

Tracey walked away, through busy passages and into open squares. She found a small café where she sat and ordered a coffee, keeping to the back out of the way of passing tourists. She had to get her thoughts together. She didn't want to contact any of her family in England. No doubt Steve would enquire of them if they'd heard from her. He would have to keep up the pretence of being at home.

Was the fire started deliberately by Steve in some bizarre way to get rid of her? With no thought of the others who would be injured?

Tracey couldn't believe that Steve would turn to arson. The church was on their tour schedule, so he knew approximately when she'd be there. She was consumed with the thought that it wasn't an accident. Why did Steve go to Paris of all places, if he was having an affair with Sally? Why go to all these lengths? What had he said to the guide? She'd find that out later.

She tried to think of how she had missed tell-tale signs of his infidelity. She had a lot of hobbies, a part-time job, household tasks to manage. That's why the garden had fallen behind being tended. She just couldn't fit it all in. How did Steve hope to explain the untidy garden away when she arrived home on Monday night?

He continually worked late, not wanting to eat when he arrived home. That had happened a lot lately. He complained that the directors wouldn't employ a manager to assist him. He had also started going to meetings in different towns, needing overnight accommodation for that. She had innocently thought that was good for the company and proved it was doing well.

Suddenly her phone rang. Instinct told her not to answer it. She saw it was Steve calling. She let it ring. He can sweat or celebrate, she didn't care which today. She was disturbed by the whole experience. What should she do? Looking around, she studied the people around her. She had been oblivious to their existence while she ruminated over her situation. There were tourists but many French people as well.

A woman stopped at her table.

'May I share your table? The café is quite busy.'

'Yes, with pleasure. You're English?'

'I live here now and speak fluent French but recognise people from home. It's an odd thing - could be dress or an aura about us English folk. What brings you here?'

'I'm visiting Paris for the weekend, on a tour. Do you work here?' Tracey wanted to take her mind off herself and her problems.

'I live here. I'm an artist and have studios on the south bank near Notre Dame. You must see the Pont Neuf, not far from here. Then you could wander up the Champs Elysee towards the Arc de Triomphe.'

Tracey nodded.

'That sounds like a good idea. How do I get to the Pont Neuf from here?'

She used her map for confirmation. Thanking the stranger, she paid her bill and left, conscious that she should really get back to the hotel and hide herself in case she bumped into Steve and Sally. However, it was a huge city and unlikely that they would bump into each other. Curiosity won and she decided to do some sightseeing on her own.

She enjoyed her walk and managed to find her way back to the hotel using her map. On approaching it, she decided to walk cautiously in case Steve and Sally were watching the entrance for her return. Not noticing them around the outside, she entered and walked up to the desk for her key. When a hand touched her shoulder, she almost screamed.

'Tracey. I am pleased to see you.' Tracey was also pleased to see Jerry, the tour guide.

'I'm concerned for your safety. We had a good tour of the city. No-one else is missing although some other tourists are. A great tragedy.'

As there was no-one else in the lobby, Tracy decided to be honest with him. They found seats in a secluded corner.

'I'm concerned that the fire may not have been an accident. I saw my husband and his female colleague in the crowd when I left the church among a group of other tourists. I observed them from the shade of a tree in the park. He sent me on this holiday, so he knew I would be here. Why come here with his lover unless to get rid of me?'

'It's up to the police and fire department to establish if it's arson. As you don't want him near you, I'll be extra vigilant and non-committal about your whereabouts. At the end of the weekend, you have to go home. You'll then find out whatever your future is going to be.'

When she arrived in her room, a note had been pushed under her door. It was from the reception staff, saying that her husband had been enquiring after her, having heard of the fire in the church and knowing that she would be visiting it.

She phoned reception and asked them not to let anyone, even her husband, know that she was alright. Just to say that they hadn't seen her and couldn't divulge any more information over the phone. She hoped the French staff would be discreet.

The rest of the weekend passed without incident. Tracey was relieved that the Sunday mystery tour destination hadn't been advertised and she could relax on the trip to Versailles. She enjoyed that last day amongst people who weren't interested in her personal life.

When she arrived home by taxi, the house was in darkness. She had expected the children to be at home. She looked in every room downstairs. All as she had left it. Looking out into the garden, that seemed the same as well. She took her suitcase upstairs and noticed that Steve's clothes were scattered around as if he had left in a hurry. She shoved them into a black bin liner which she found in the bathroom cupboard, as well as his dirty washing that was still in the wash basket.

'That's just the start', she thought.

She decided to telephone her sister.

'Hi, Joan, how are you?'

'Tracey? Is it really you? Steve phoned to say he'd received a phone call that you were missing in a fire in Paris and had to go to find you.'

'Are the boys ok? I hope they aren't worried. I'll come to fetch them now.' She avoided mentioning Paris to her sister. She would prefer to show her the evidence on her phone.

'Steve said he'd only be back on Tuesday. I've fed them and they have their clothes here for school. I'll get them packed up. Have a bit of supper and a chat while you're here.'

Tracey agreed. She left the house locked and in darkness, just in case Steve had lied about when he'd be home.

The boys were pleased to see her and gave her huge hugs. They were unaware of the events in Paris.

'Is it ok if we stay to finish our game with Paul and Simon?' Peter was keen on anything to delay the thought of school the next day.

'Yes, Aunt Joan and I will have a chat in the kitchen. Not too much noise, now. You don't want to disturb Uncle Tom while he watches the football.' She left Peter and Charlie with their cousins.

While Joan made her a cup of tea and prepared some food, she chatted about their weekend and how they'd all had a lot of fun.

'I was surprised that Steve rushed off to Paris like that at the drop of a hat. Bank holidays are certainly not the time to easily get transport and accommodation. Are you sure you didn't see him?' She placed a plate of food in front of Tracey.

Tracey had left her phone with the picture of Steve and Sally, on the table for Joan to see.

'Yes, I did see him and with Sally. That was when we were evacuated from the church. It was horrible in there when we first smelled the smoke and the alarm went off. Everyone just rushed out. I noticed them and instinctively didn't want them to see me. I don't know why. The crowd took me along with them into the park where I stood beside a tree, watching them. I also

53

kept an eye open for our tour guide, Jerry, as I was sure he would need to do a head count. I did phone him to let him know I was safe and warned him against letting anyone else know. I told him someone was there who I didn't want to see. Later, back at the hotel, I told him why I'd acted like that. Joan, how come Steve and Sally were there, right outside that church, as if waiting to see if I was going to be dead? Do you think he is capable of arson to get rid of me? It's bizarre, I know but it looks odd.'

Joan was shocked by all that Tracey had told her.

'No, I can't believe anything like this of Steve. If you hadn't shown me those photos, I wouldn't believe you. It seems that he's having an affair. I can't understand why he went to all that trouble of buying you that holiday in Paris and then going there himself with his new love? Did you have any inkling that he had someone else?'

'No, I just thought he was tired out with work. However, I spent a lot of time thinking about little things and some big things as well, this weekend. His sudden need to spend nights away on business. Working late and not needing a meal when he arrived home. The odd occasion when I used his car, finding a lipstick or earrings that definitely weren't mine. He always had a feasible explanation for their presence.'

'So, do you have any idea what you're going to do now?'

'I've already put all his dirty washing in a black bin bag. He can take it with him when I throw him out when he gets home. Thanks for not saying anything to the boys about me potentially being missing. I did wonder if he'd contacted you. I didn't want to phone you myself to put you in an awkward situation, lying to him. I just turned my phone off and ignored it.'

'Look. You know where I am if you need my help or an ear to bend. Just look after yourself and make sure you and the boys are fine.'

'Don't worry, I intend to. I think I'll take them home now, so long as they've finished their game.' Almost on cue, the boys came into the kitchen. Paul and Simon told their mum they were all starving. She gave them a packet of crisps each, a small drink, then fetched Peter and Charlie's belongings.

As Tracey and the boys left, Joan gave Tracey a big hug. 'You know where I am.'

Tracey thanked her for having the boys. They gave their aunt a big hug, shook their uncle's hand while Tracey gave him a hug as well as her nephews. She didn't know what the next few days would bring but she would live up to her surname.

When they arrived home, the house lights were on. Tracey sat in the car on the drive and didn't move for a minute. Peter and Charlie started to open the car door but she stopped them.

'Boys, can you just wait here a minute. I want to see if that's your Dad indoors. I left the house in darkness and Aunt Joan said he was only coming home tomorrow.'

She walked slowly to the front door. It was unlocked. Carefully opening it, she walked in. Not saying anything, she looked into the lounge as she passed, then the dining room and entered the kitchen. Sitting slumped at the table, covered in blood, was Steve. A knife was on the table.

She left the house, got back into the car and rushed back to Joan's house. The boys were terrified as they hadn't seen their mother lose her cool before.

Joan and Tom welcomed her back, astounded by what she had to say. They immediately took the boys in hand and left Tracey for a minute in the kitchen. Joan and Tom decided that Joan would go back with Tracey and ring the police.

Tracey didn't want to go back into the kitchen. Joan just looked at the scene from the door. When the police arrived there were many questions, late into the night. They advised Tracey to leave the house while they did their forensic examinations. She was allowed to get some clothing from the bedroom, in the presence of a female police officer and left a set of keys for them to lock up when they were finished.

Now, it could look like Tracey hadn't told the truth, that Steve was at home when she returned and murdered him in a rage.

After months of enquiries and examinations, interviews with Sally, the tour guide, Jerry, the French hotelier, Steve's directors, Tracey, Joan and Tom, the true picture was revealed.

Sally had enticed Steve to book the weekend in Paris while Tracey was there. She had engineered their visit to the church to coincide with Tracey's tour. They had visited the church earlier. When Steve thought she was lighting a candle at one of the sconces, she was actually starting a small fire under a pew. The fire in the church was arson created by Sally not Steve.

When Steve had realised that Tracey was possibly dead, he found he really did love her and didn't want to leave her or cause her any harm. Sally couldn't take that when he told her. They cut short their stay in Paris. Arriving by taxi at Steve's house, they found the family car was missing. Steve told her it was over between them. She went into a rage, grabbed the first knife she could find in a drawer and stabbed him while he sat at the table, head in hands with shame at what he had been doing to his family. She had committed the murder.

Tracey was glad she hadn't let her sons go into the house to see the mess Sally had left. They took a while to recover but with support from their family, they managed to. And Tracey?

When life had settled down after Steve's funeral, the inquest and the murder trial, Tracey went on another touring holiday on her own. Amazingly, Jerry was the tour guide. He was not married. They became good friends and the future looked brighter for the whole family.

Spring

He strode eagerly down the street, almost marching as if he was in the army.

A smart man who everyone could trust. This would be the final choir practice afternoon followed by a tea party before he moved away.

No-one knew his dark side. The nightly online dealings as Sammy Smith, when he lured other pensioners into bogus investments. He inwardly chuckled. Far removed from Michael Pendennis.

His years in the Paymaster's office had been beneficial. Names accumulated then had generated a steady supplementary income. The weekend would see him with exotic Mellita in Myanmar starting a new life.

The Arsonist

He watched the fires burning on the hills in the distance. They had spread quickly.

He was alarmed when the fires drew near the houses. The firemen managed to dowse the surrounding area. Farmers dug trenches so the fire wouldn't spread on the dry grass.

When his parents related how wonderful it was to see the fires on the moors during the Queen's Sixtieth Jubilee, he wondered what it would look like from their home.

Now he knew. He wished he hadn't started it. Too scared to own up, he shut himself in his bedroom - his self-imposed punishment.

The Arrests

It was early and still dark. Gordon heard a milkman. He stayed out of sight.

Bobby had said three a.m. He was late. It'd taken months to set this up. Gordon heard a low whistle. He stepped out. Three men approached quietly. He reached into his pocket for the money. One grabbed his hand.

'No funny business.'

'Show me the stuff.'

'Give us the cash.'

'No goods, no cash.'

'Brave talk. Show him.'

Another produced the package.

Gordon passed over the money, pressing a hidden buzzer.

Lights blazed. Police everywhere.

Shouts of 'You scum.'

Gordon grinned and walked away.

Untold Family Stories

Blimey. There he goes again, walking past the prison. Why does he do it?

This is the third day he's done that, pacing outside the gates, looking up as if expecting something to happen, then walking away again to the park.

Mum used to wander but Dad is worse. He seems to have a problem with this prison, yet I don't recall anyone mentioning that someone we know had been in there.

As usual, I followed him at a distance and once I saw he had settled on his favourite bench in the park, I nipped into the shop for our bits of groceries. He was walking past the door as I came out. I acted surprised to see him and we walked home together.

Not knowing how best to broach the subject, I asked if he had enjoyed his walk. He was hesitant in replying and said he was bothered by something from years ago but couldn't recall what it was. I told him it would come to him eventually. He asked if I had looked through all Mum's papers since she'd passed on. I said I thought I had, although there were some things in the attic I hadn't yet had a chance to look at.

We ate our lunch and Dad dozed while I tidied up. As he seemed quite settled, I decided to see if there was anything of importance in the old boxes and bags. I ended up bringing a load of things down into the spare bedroom, sneezing from the accumulated dust.

Looking in a bag, I found old clothing that should've gone to the dump, although looking at it again, I wondered if one of those vintage type shops might like them. Putting the bag to one side to attend to later, I looked in a shoe box. At first it seemed to be full of photos. People I recognised from years ago, Gran and Grandad, Mum when she was small and me growing up. The usual collection of family special occasions recorded on black and white film. At the bottom of the box were a couple of envelopes.

Keeping a keen ear on any sounds from downstairs, I decided to see what was inside. They were all addressed to Mum but typed. The postmark was local as well. Opening the first envelope, I saw that it was a letter from the prison. I gasped when I saw Dad's name in the subject heading. The letter informed Mum that Dad was due for a review of his sentence as he had served four of the five years for which he had been imprisoned. It was likely that he would be allowed out on parole as he had been an ideal inmate, not causing or being involved in any bother. I looked at the date. It was 1950, two years before I was born.

My heart was racing as I wondered what was in the next envelope. It was a letter from Dad to Mum, the year before, telling Mum that he was now a qualified electrician, having been trained in the prison, so when he was released, he'd be able to get a good job to provide for her. He also said he was constantly thinking about who stitched him up and would most likely never know but things would be different when he came home.

There was no mention of Mum visiting him at all.

Dad had worked for the same firm of electricians all my life. I had been well cared for by my parents and there was never any hint of this period. Like so many things in many families, the bad stuff is tucked away hopefully never to surface again. Mum must have forgotten about these items and then when her memory started to fail her, she wouldn't have thought about them at all.

I took the box downstairs and placed it on the dining room table. Dad had stirred, so I put the kettle on and pondered what to say to him. I couldn't just let it lie, especially as that period of his life seemed to be bothering him.

I told him that I'd been in the attic while he was sleeping and found some bags of things and a few boxes which I'd brought down to the spare room. He frowned then carried on with his drink. I told him about the clothing in one bag and what I intended doing. He told me to look in pockets before I washed them. Surprised, I said I would. Then I told him about the photos and lastly the letters in the same box. His eyes took on a distant look and I let him think about it, waiting for a reaction.

'That bloody witch', he said.

'Who are you talking about, Dad?'

'Not your Mum, if that's what bothers you. No, her sister. She had this fella who was going to be the bees' knees. Swaggering thing he was. She was besotted with him. She came one day and asked if I'd help him move some things but it had to be at night as that's the only time he could use the van from work. I didn't ask what things and your Mum just wanted me to help her as it seemed important. It'd also bring in some cash.'

'On the night, we got to the pottery where Jimmy worked and all the boxes were stacked ready for moving. I didn't see anything wrong as it looked organised, in fact the thought that it was untoward never entered my head. We got the boxes loaded up and I was on the way out the gates, when all hell broke loose. That Jimmy had been in his own car and I couldn't see sight nor sound of him. Two police cars parked in front of me and a van full of policemen stopped behind them, with their batons swinging. They yelled for everyone to get out. I climbed down from the truck and said it was only me and I had been helping a mate to move some things. They said they were all stolen, so I was nicked. I tried to prove my innocence but we couldn't afford a lawyer and Jimmy was never found again. Your Aunt Susan went away soon after and I have a sneaky suspicion that she went off with him. Your Mum didn't see her again, as far as I know.'

I had so many questions flying around in my head but didn't want to upset him, as he was getting angry yet I knew that while he was remembering now, he may not in a few days' time.

I plucked up courage and asked what was in the boxes.

'It was a special edition of crockery for the gentry in a country house somewhere in Scotland; inlaid with gold leaf and the works, evidently.'

Dad wouldn't have known anything about that kind of stuff as he worked for the council as a bin man at the time. Another thing I didn't know.

'Someone in the pottery must have seen Jimmy doing what he shouldn't during the day and spoke to management, who decided to keep an eye on developments and that's why I was caught.'

Mum and especially her family were devastated but Mum stuck by him, knowing what had happened from the beginning. Aunt Susan, who I had never heard of before, was their darling daughter, so it was harder for my grandparents to bear the loss.

Dad then started to get upset, as he thought of all the years he and Mum had been separated, all because they tried to help out and earn a few more bob. I soothed him, telling him that he and Mum were the best parents anyone could wish for and he had never let me down.

I spared him the knowledge that there was another envelope with letters from Susan to Mum but Mum had never answered them. I gleaned that information from what Aunt Susan had written. Susan and Jimmy stayed togethcr but were always on the move and then the letters stopped, three years after Dad had been imprisoned.

I made us a fresh cup of tea and mentally decided that I would look through everything when Dad was in bed.

I decided to take the bags of clothing downstairs first, so I could give them a good shake outside. I then examined them for damage and to decide what to do with each item. Had there been moths present, I'd have chucked the lot. I lay each garment on the table. Some looked like they could've been Gran's clothes but possibly Mum's from when she was younger.

Remembering Dad's suggestion of looking through the pockets, I examined them thoroughly. Dresses were put in one pile, not worth hanging up before I washed them. In one skirt pocket I found a folded piece of paper, an old shopping list. That made me smile. The skirts joined the pile of dresses. Two jackets were the only outer clothing in the bags. One had nothing in the pockets. A camel jacket looked good. I put it on for size. A bit musty but could be dry cleaned to freshen it up. I felt in the pocket, expecting to find a scarf. What I pulled out was a man's handkerchief with a beautiful brooch wrapped in it. No jewellery box and no note. A spray of five flowers with stones of different colours in them. I'd never seen it before. I put it to one side to ask Dad about it in the morning.

I then had a thorough look through the box I had brought downstairs to show Dad. I read every letter again, then folded them into the original envelopes. I hadn't reached the bottom of the box in the afternoon, so was excited to see what else was in there.

Under the envelope I had already looked through with Susan's letters, was a long thin letter. It was from a solicitor in southern Spain, informing Mum of Aunt Susan's death. I looked at the date, horrified to see it was a year before Mum had become ill. So fairly recent. It requested that Mum should write to confirm receipt of the letter, as there was information to her benefit in the solicitor's hands. Nothing indicated that Mum had replied. I wondered if I should approach Dad about that in the morning.

I sat and thought about the events of the past four years, the letter being dated five years ago. When Mum had started with her dementia, Dad had asked me if I could help him look after her. They were both in their late seventies, I was widowed and my two children had lives of their own. Although I had a part-time job, it was not necessary for me to work. Being an only child, there was no-one else to help them and I was pleased to have something worthwhile to do. Mum didn't mention any of the family issues. She had helped Dad clear out the spare room before I moved back after arranging for my house to be rented out. He would've carried the bags into the attic after she packed them up. No wonder she couldn't cope with anything regarding Susan. Dad wouldn't have wanted anything to do with it.

I was amazed to see it was after midnight, so tidied the paperwork away, leaving the solicitor's letter at the top, moved the clothing to deal with first thing in the morning and headed for bed.

Unusually for me, I overslept. When I walked into the kitchen, Dad was sitting at the table looking at the clothing piled on the floor.

'Your Mum's best dresses, those were. She couldn't part with them. Loved to see her in that blue one with the tiny white flowers on it. Matched her eyes.'

'Sorry, Dad, I've overslept and meant to have washed those before you got up.'

'No bother, lass, you deserve a rest once in a while. Did you find anything more interesting?'

'Shall we get breakfast first, Dad? Then we can mull over all this other stuff.'

'No, I'd rather find out what you've come across, as I'm sure there must be something. Just by the way you are looking at me, as if I'm a piece of china that's going to break. Oh, I know I'm old and forgetful, memory not what it should be but some things jerk it back into life. Let's be having it then.'

I smiled at his candour and sat down at the table.

'You see that camel coat I've put on the chair? It belonged to Mum, didn't it?'

Dad nodded.

'Well, you told me to look in all the pockets. I found a shopping list in a skirt pocket, which amused me. It's here, in Mum's handwriting. Then I tried that jacket on. Feeling in the pocket, thinking a scarf was in there, I found this.'

I took the handkerchief out of my cardigan pocket.

'Do you recognise this handkerchief, Dad?'

'It's mine. I had a set of four like that but one went missing. Your Mum said I must have dropped it somewhere. I knew I hadn't.'

'Well, there's something wrapped inside it. Look. Have you seen this before?'

Dad looked at the piece of jewellery, sparkling in the morning light. For a while he didn't speak and I gave him time to think about it.

'You know, your Mum was a bit queer around the time the hanky went missing. She was a bit upset one day when I came home from work but said it was just a woman's thing, feeling her age and not knowing what to do about it. Over the next few days, she seemed to be distracted. One of the neighbours mentioned she'd had a female visitor, all dressed up but your Mum denied it. I wonder if it was Susan. Now that you have found that, Susan could have given that to her and she didn't want to show it to me as she knew I'd chuck it. Have it if you want it, or give it to your Kath.'

'Thanks, Dad. I certainly won't 'chuck' it. But this leads me on to something else I found. A letter from a solicitor in Spain, a year before Mum's dementia set in. The letter informed Mum of Susan's death. Do you know about that?'

'Yes and I told her not to do it. If there was any money it would most probably be stolen and I didn't want her involved in any profits from ill-gotten gains.'

'So Mum didn't contact the solicitor?'

'Not unless she did it behind my back. Best to chuck that letter, as I thought your Mum had.'

'I'll put it away for now, Dad. We'll get on with our breakfast and the rest of our day.'

I decided to put the box and its contents in my room in my wardrobe for safe-keeping. I had thoughts of Dad burning everything. I didn't know if raking up the past was going to affect him in any way.

We had a visit from my son, Sean, at the weekend. He sometimes came round with his girlfriend but on this occasion was on his own. Dad enjoyed his company and they chatted away in the lounge while I prepared lunch. After lunch when Dad went to rest, Sean mentioned the conversation he and my Dad had been having.

'Gramps says you've been digging up the family's murky past. Lots of mysteries there. What are you going to do about it?'

'How much did he tell you?'

'All about the mysterious Aunt Susan and her boyfriend, his spell in prison, you finding that brooch and the letter from the solicitor. I think you should find out what the letter was all about.'

'Sean, I live with Gramps and don't want him to be hurt. If I receive letters here from Spain, it may upset him. You're a lawyer. Would you look into it? I must admit, I am curious beyond belief. Just hope it doesn't mean that we'll be stung for money she owes people.'

'I'll do that, Mum but don't worry about hurting Gramps. He told me that it's all water under the bridge now and we may as well know Susan's story.'

'He said that? Well, well. I'm amazed. I won't say anything to him unless he brings it up.'

Sean left in the early evening with the solicitor's letter.

Over the next few weeks, Dad and I got on with our daily routine. I took the clothes, once cleaned, to the charity shop apart from the camel coat which I fancied for myself. After having it cleaned, it looked as good as new.

Sean invited Dad and I to visit him at work one Friday and to book into a hotel overnight as a little break. This was odd but Dad seemed all for it. It was only an hour's journey to Liverpool for us. The hotel was near the Albert Dock and Dad was looking forward to sitting and watching activity in the Mersey after we'd visited Sean. I parked at the hotel and we took a taxi to Sean's office. I didn't want to tire Dad with walking.

Sean met us in reception and took us to a meeting room. He told us what he had found out.

'Susan and Jimmy had parted company a few years after they went to Spain. Susan became tired of living in constant fear of him being caught as he carried on with his wheeling and dealing. She didn't get involved with any of it, worked in a restaurant and could support herself. A lot of the time it was her money that kept a roof over their heads. She was good at the restaurant business, got promoted to management and ran a chain of restaurants for Carlos Diaz. When his wife passed away, Carlos asked her to marry him. He didn't have any children and wanted to know that the business would carry on for all his loyal customers. Before he passed away, he advised her to sell the business while it was a going concern and help the new owners to settle in. She did that, then found that she was terminally ill with cancer. About that time, she visited Gran, so that's when she must have given Gran that brooch. She left her villa and all her money to Gran. Gran would have had to go to Spain to claim it.'

'Now, as it stands, you and Gramps, are Gran's next of kin. The money and villa are yours but you will have to visit Spain to claim it. Otherwise the Spanish state gets it ten years after Aunt Susan died.'

'So Susan turned out to be a better person after all that? And I didn't let Mary have anything to do with her. How wrong of me.'

'Gramps, you had lost years because of Aunt Susan's boyfriend. If she'd stayed to defend you, things would've been very different. As it is, she tried to make amends this way for all the wrong she did then. I think we should all go to Spain, have a chat with the solicitor and see what can be done.'

'I can't go. I'm too old and haven't got a passport.'

'We're in Liverpool, Gramps. I've got it all sorted for a photographer to take your photos and we can visit the passport office today. It will take a week for the passport to come back. Mum has a valid passport.'

'I'll only go if Kath can come with us. She should have some of that enjoyment as well.'

I was amazed that Dad was willing to go abroad on what might turn out to be a wild goose chase. However, if Sean had understood the solicitor correctly, we might have a permanent holiday home in Spain. This could be good for Dad.

'I've already spoken with Kath. As soon as your passport comes back, we'll book the flights and accommodation. We'll all enjoy it and think of Gran and Aunt Susan.'

Dad was eager but voiced a few regrets when we were wandering along the harbourside. He was sad that Mum hadn't let on about Aunt Susan seeing her. She was such a caring person, taking his feelings into consideration all the time.

'That was Mum, Dad. She cared for both of us and wouldn't hurt anyone. I'm sure she'll be looking down on us and enjoying what she is seeing.'

'Wonder what happened to that Jimmy?'

'Sean told me he passed away in jail. The authorities eventually caught up with him and he had a tougher sentence in Spain than he would have had in the UK.'

'He got his just deserts then.'

Everything was as Sean had understood it. Dad inherited Mum's legacy. He signed the villa over to Sean and Kath, with the proviso that Dad and I could holiday there as often as we wanted. Dad enjoyed feeling the warm sun, avoiding periods of intense heat. He also was free of financial worries for the rest of his life.

Aunt Susan was forgiven, at last.

Bad Memories

Fifty years after that unforgettable experience, William recalled the events leading to his family's move.

The family had gathered for his grandmother's ninetieth birthday. A great party was had until loud voices came from the kitchen. The back door slammed. Mother came in tearful to phone for help. Aunty Linda followed holding a bloody knife. Gran fainted.

Uncle Alf had tried to protect Mother who was being bullied by Dad, who had grabbed the knife, stabbed Uncle Alf then run away.

William's Dad was arrested and imprisoned. Uncle Alf and Gran died. They never saw Dad again, till now.

The Shooting

A crowd had gathered at the scene.

Albert Johns was dead.

Fred became Albert's dealer when his mother had terminal cancer. Albert's drug empire was failing. Police had arrested most of the gang. Fred double crossed him.

Albert wanted revenge. He arranged to meet Fred. As Albert pulled the trigger to shoot Fred, another shot rang out. Fred clutched his arm, Albert fell. Another shot was heard. Fred's mother had turned his father's gun on herself. Fred was alive but wounded. Ambulances and police arrived.

Fred was arrested for dealing and hospitalised for treatment, devastated at his mother's suicide.

Umbrella Mystery

Strangers passing on a crowded street. People hurrying with many things to do.

She watched while waiting. One woman dropped her umbrella. A man picked it up. The woman turned to look at him. Their eyes met. He turned away. He carried on walking with the umbrella. The woman walked away.

The watcher was intrigued. Who to watch now? A screech of brakes. The woman jumped into a car.

The man ran towards the tube station. Two men apprehended him. The umbrella flew into the air. Official looking papers fell out of it.

The lengths newspaper reporters go to.

Tough Lives

'She certainly doesn't deserve all the hassle those children have given her throughout their lives.' The neighbours were concerned as they saw the police car draw up outside Jean's house.

Jean had worked hard to keep her family together when her husband died after falling from a high level on a building site. The accident investigators found that he hadn't worn appropriate safety equipment. She'd always maintained that the company didn't provide enough barriers around the scaffolding for the workers. They were soon put up after Tommy died.

Her eldest son, John, had mixed with a bad lot when he was at school. He thought he was helping his Mum by earning extra money but ended up in prison after he was caught transporting drugs on his bicycle. She had no idea he was doing it but after it all came out, odd things fell into place. He'd tell her the greengrocer had given them a bit extra in the shopping he did for her. Sweets sometimes turned up out of nowhere for the little ones. He was due out in six months' time. He'd been using the time in prison to study maths and English and wanted to go to college when he came home, to learn a trade.

Her middle son, Philip, got hooked on drugs at school.

'It's just a bit of fun, Mum, nothing serious.'

'I still don't want you doing it. You'll get into trouble and where are you getting the money from to pay for the stuff?'

'No need to worry, Mum. It pays for itself.' However, he ended up in a psychiatric hospital. Hopefully he'd be straight when he came out in two years' time.

Jean couldn't see him very often as he was in a different area of the country. The rail fares were too expensive. Coaches took too long and required an overnight stay somewhere. Her brother took her once every three months. At the last visit, Philip looked a lot better.

'I've enjoyed reading all sorts of books, Mum. Really got into it. I've enquired about studying and they're going to let me know.' Jean didn't enquire too much about what it was he was going to study. She didn't know whether to believe him or not.

Jean was still keeping her job down in the Council offices. Some of her colleagues frowned on her. Most of the team she worked in were very supportive.

She hoped and prayed the twins would turn out better. Susan was doing well at school with her commercial subjects. She hated PE but loved playing tennis in the summer. Norman was a studious boy, who always had some kind of scientific book under his nose. She'd seen him on the internet on the odd occasion but always shut the sites down when she went into the dining room. They could only afford one computer and everyone had to have access to it.

Jean was shocked to be called to the school, just when she was beginning to think that things may be settling down.

Mr Warren was kind to Jean when she arrived in his office.

'I know this is going to be a shock to you, Mrs Mason. You've had more than your fair share of problems to deal with alone. Norman has been an ideal student up to now. However, he's been trying to access military sites on the school computer which the children are allowed to use at lunch times.'

'Oh, no, surely not. What for?'

'He told us he wanted to make a bomb, just to see if he could get it to explode. Norman has broken the school rules on computer use. Norman is to be excluded from school while the police undertake investigations.'

'The police? Oh, not again. Not another one.' She was distraught. 'I had such high hopes for Norman. He's very studious and seems to want to be different from his brothers. What are the police going to do?'

'After our meeting, the officers want to interview you. Firstly, we're also disappointed in this discovery. We cannot allow Norman's actions to go unpunished.'

'His GCSE's are coming up. Can he still sit them? I can't take time off work to supervise him at home as we need the money.'

'That was the second point I was coming to. I'm going to have a word with the officer and see if we can have a probation officer present in school to keep an eye on his activities.'

'I'd be ever so grateful if he could finish his studies. I'm really sorry that this has happened. I don't know if I could've stopped it.'

'In years gone by, children blew up garden sheds with the small scientific kits they received for birthdays. The world has changed now and this is no longer acceptable.' Mr Warren felt sorry for Jean as he knew she'd struggled to keep her children on a straight path.

He called the officer into the office.

'Mrs Mason, this is Sergeant Trent. Sergeant, Mrs Mason had no idea Norman was researching anything like this. We've discussed the possibility of Norman having a probation officer supervise him at school.'

'We'll have to let the court decide on that and it depends on what we find on his home computer. I understand that Norman has use of a computer at home?'

'Yes, he does. He and his sister, Susan, share the use of it as we can't afford two. Will that have to go away as well? What about Susan's work? How is she going to manage?'

'We'll sort that out somehow, Mrs Mason' interjected Mr Warren seeing Jean getting more distressed. 'We'll have another discussion in a few days, once we know more. Until then, I'm sorry but Norman has to stay away from school.

The police took Jean and Norman home, then took the computer away so they could examine it. Jean was ashamed when the neighbours looked to see what was happening.

When Susan arrived home, Jean had a long, quiet conversation with her. She obtained assurances from Susan that her life was going well.

'I want to do something good with my life. I'm not getting into anything illegal at school or anywhere else. I don't want to spoil my chances of making a success of any future employment. I miss John and Philip and am glad that Norman doesn't have to go away. I don't want to be a worry to you, Mum. I want to help you.' Jean hugged her and held back her tears.

Jean had a long conversation with Norman as well.

'What have you been up to, Norman? Is this why you shut down the computer so many times when I enter the dining room?'

'If it's available on the internet, why can't I access it? I don't mean any harm.'

It was going to take a long time to get him to see her point of view. She reminded him of how it was when he had been to see John in jail. How ashamed he'd felt visiting his brother there.

'Your perceived innocent actions are in fact huge misdemeanours in this day and age, when terrorism is so rife. I hope once you have had all your interviews with the police, the education authorities and anyone else who may become involved, that you'll see the error of your ways. I don't mind telling you, Norman, that I'm very disappointed in this development.'

Between the three of them while sitting around the table at home, they discussed the subject of how best to be law abiding citizens.

'You're really clever and good at physics and maths, Norman. You could win a bursary to go to university and play legally with ammunition and firearms.' Susan was complimentary to Norman whilst also showing her horror at his actions.

'I didn't think you took much interest in me. You seem more interested in social work and how you could make other people's lives better.'

'I'll start by practicing my mentoring on you.' They all laughed which relieved the tension in the house.

Jean asked Norman to promise that he wouldn't get mixed up in websites or anything that would ruin his chances of a good future.

The road ahead looked tough. Jean could see that. She could only hope that Norman would keep his promises and the authorities would look kindly on him.

How she missed the support her husband could have given her.

Crime Doesn't Pay

All this activity left her with a splitting headache.

She'd witnessed the man run from the chemist shop into the road. The lorry had no time to stop. Someone from the shop ran out, shouting, to stop him.

Suddenly, police car and ambulance sirens sounded. Two ambulances and four police cars pulled up. The man lay dead still on the road. The lorry driver climbed down from his cab, in shock.

'I couldn't stop.'

Officers approached onlookers for witnesses, including the woman, sickened by what she'd seen. They said the man had stolen drugs. She urgently needed them now.

The Disposal

Once they agreed on the disposal, they went to work.

Joe had trained as a butcher. He knew the best way to cut to avoid a bloody mess.

Thick sheets were laid out on the wide table. All three lifted the still form onto the table. A dead weight. Joe unwrapped his tools.

In no time, Joe had detached the limbs and started on the torso. Harry bagged up the manageable joints while Tom sealed each package securely.

Tom packed them in the prepared boxes.

There was enough meat to keep their families fed for a while. Poor deer.

Gigantic Help

On assessing the damage to the car, he decided to walk for help. His phone wasn't receiving a signal. He'd noticed lights on at a house he'd passed not too far away.

There were no streetlights this far out of town, in the hills. His eyes soon became accustomed to the dark, moonlight shining through the trees helped him. He approached the entrance to the property with confidence and was hopeful of being able to phone for help. This would happen tonight of all nights. An animal running in front of him causing him to brake suddenly and swerve, resulting in him ending up with his front left wheel in a ditch. There was no sign of the animal, which had most probably bolted.

He knocked on the door. There was silence everywhere. In the distance an owl hooted. All of a sudden, the door was flung open and a huge man stood in the doorway.

'What do you want at this hour?'

Peter explained his predicament.

'No telephones in this house. Don't believe in them. I'll get the pony and trap and take you back to your car. See if we can pull it out of the ditch.'

Peter felt like he had gone back in time. Pony and trap? No telephones?

The man brought out a lantern, lit with a candle. Peter was beginning to accept the weirdness of the situation. He introduced himself but the man seemed totally disinterested in personal contact. They walked around the side of the house to a barn, where the man slid back the bolt to reveal a well-maintained trap and a pony in a stall. He hitched the pony to the trap, told Peter to climb on and they started on the journey.

There was no conversation as they rode along. Peter longed to ask more about this man. When they arrived at Peter's car, the man looked around it, assessed what needed to be done and told Peter to stand clear. The man stepped into the ditch and with one big heave, lifted the front of the car back onto the road. Peter was amazed. There appeared to be only superficial damage to the car.

The man accepted his thanks and told Peter to drive more carefully in future, calling the car an infernal modern contraption.

Peter arrived at his meeting slightly late and feeling tense from his experience getting there. He was pleased he was staying the night and not having to drive that road again in the dark.

The next day he took the same route home, wanting to see the exact spot where the car had left the road. He couldn't find it. There were no marks on the bank at the spot where he thought he'd come off. He looked out for the house. The only one he came across was a large modern mansion with electrical gates.

Talking to his colleagues when he was next in the office, they told him the strange story of a circus performer who had allegedly murdered his family in the nineteenth century. Most people who were raised in that area were brought up with the legend.

He had been a huge man, performing many feats with his strong-arm tactics. He had inherited the house when his parents passed away. His brother and sisters remained living in it. He considered them to be parasites. They were never seen after he moved in. When he died, their remains were found in trunks in what must have been the siblings' bedrooms. Once all the remains were removed from the house, it had mysteriously burnt down.

Evidently, the people who bought the property and built on it, kept the barn and the trap, any animals having died soon after their master.

Peter shivered when told this story, wondering how he could have had such a strange experience.

His car still had the dent in the wheel arch to prove his part of the story.

Prison Walls

It feels like forever that I have walked outside these walls, waiting for them to let him go. People say he's a no-good son. He was always good to Elsie and me. Never let us do anything that was too burdensome. Never let us carry our shopping when it was heavy. Was good at schoolwork and got a good job on the council when he left school.

It threw Elsie and me when the police called to say he'd been arrested. Some charge of drug dealing that had been going on for years. We couldn't believe it. Our lad doing that. He didn't seem to have funny moods that you associate with these stories. We didn't see the people he socialised with down the pub. Never heard neighbours say ought against him.

Elsie insisted on going to the trial. I was against it. Knew it would upset her. Soon as they sent him down, proved guilty, she fainted. Hit her head against the woodwork and was in hospital five days before she passed on. What a to-do that all was. They let him serve his time in the local prison. What good that did, I wouldn't know, 'cept easier for me to see him. Think his Mum's death really shook him. Couldn't stop apologising when I visited. Police escort to

Elsie's funeral in handcuffs. Really ashamed of him, I was.

Soon as he's out, we'll be away from here and that gang we found he was involved with. Now I'm kicking stones as I walk. Stumble along most days. Knocked on the pokey door of the big gates just now. They said he's not coming home for another two months. Must have got the dates mixed up when he said last visit. And I had his favourite food ready for him – that poppy seed loaf and a good beef stew, with poppy seed cake to follow.

Will have to eat it myself.

The Loser

How did it go?

You lost control. Everything got on top of you. You decided to end it all.

Others went to Beachy Head. You chose the steep cliffs of Babbacombe Bay. You raced your car to the edge. It flew into the air but not for long. You landed, shocked. There had been a landslide. The soil was soft.

Rescuers risked their lives to save you. A helicopter winched you to safety.

Your debts were worse. There was a way out. You became a drug mule.

Your debts were cleared. You were caught.

Contemplate your future in prison.

The Weed

'I'm fed up with the way Scarlet picks on us when we're only here for the fresh air and company. We're not budding Monty Dons.'

Penny and Hilary were picked on constantly for not planting out seedlings precisely as they'd been ordered to. They regarded their volunteer gardening in the park as a pleasure; a means to meet other people and have a laugh in the fresh air.

They resolved to wind up the bossy supervisor.

'Penny, I know where we can get some 'weed'. We could smuggle it in and plant it amongst the marigold seedlings in the tunnel.'

'Great idea, Hilary. We'll do it next week.'

Some weeks passed before Annabel, thinking they were weeds, pulled one up and noticed the strange smell. She took them to Scarlet who recognised the smell as cannabis.

Everyone thought it was hilarious, except Scarlet. She called the police.

'We'll take the plants away to destroy them,' said the local PC when she had arrived, examined the plants and interviewed the gardeners.

'Aren't you going to investigate how it got into this charity plot, in a locked nursery?' Scarlet expected more from the police.

'All your volunteers have assured me they know nothing about it. Someone in a neighbouring plot could have planted them amongst the marigold seedlings. It's petty and not worth the time.'

The PC walked away with the bag containing the plants.

Scarlet was livid at the answer.

Hilary and Penny joked with the others as they resumed their tasks.

'We could have grown that stuff on and had a real party at Christmas, couldn't we, Scarlet? Or Mary could have taken some home to spice up our cookies for next week?'

The others laughed, especially at Scarlet's scowls as she walked to the office.

The Walk

The group climbed the hill to see the Bushmen's paintings on the rock. Some places were steep, other parts of the path were narrow with sheer drops to one side.

The guide led from the front, checking at intervals on the people at the rear. The couple who'd argued into the night kept apart from each other. The view from the rock was brilliant in the morning sunshine. On the way back to the hotel, they stopped to look at the protea tree, which clung perilously to the edge of the path. Its bark was blackened from the controlled burning of the vegetation earlier in the year. Someone shouted that there was a warthog on the path in front. There was a rush of movement to look at it, followed by an horrendous scream.

The man involved in the argument had slipped and was clinging to an outcrop of the root, legs floundering in mid-air.

The guide tried to form a chain of men to pull him to safety but the ground started to give way. The man fell down into the ravine, screaming as he went. His partner was ashen faced, not believing what had happened.

She'd wished him dead the previous evening. Reality today was a different story. Had anyone noticed her giving him the little push?

Turning to look around her, only one face looked at her accusingly. The guide ... her future looked bleak.

Poison Revenge

They hadn't said how the woman had died. Sandy had watched all the proceedings from beside a shop window.

The woman had collapsed on the pavement at the top of the stairs leading from the underground. A man had called an ambulance. The crew confirmed she was dead when they arrived but noticed a small amount of blood around her neck from a puncture wound. They couldn't see any obvious item that had caused it. They noted her name from the contents of her handbag, which they had placed in a plastic bag and handed to the police.

The female constable and a detective sergeant organised Marilla's body to be taken to the morgue. They had examined the cordoned off area down the stairs and around the pavement. They noted where CCTV was situated. They would retrieve footage for their investigations.

After the body was moved the constable noticed something glinting on the pavement. A hairpin which hadn't been noticed previously. She picked it up with gloved hands and placed it in an evidence bag. Soon afterwards they left in a police car.

Sandy knew they would find a minute trace of the poison on the tips of the hairpin but no finger marks. Even if they tried to find her from the CCTV footage, they would have a tough time as she couldn't wait to get rid of the wig she was wearing. She'd also change her clothing in the department store toilets and would dump the old stuff when she was out of town.

At last she had avenged her son's death.

The Accident

Before she could tell him not to get out of the car, he'd opened the door.

She'd stopped to be sick. Her stomach was wound up over the awful time she had endured last night. Andrew had embarrassed her with his insulting comments about her amongst his work colleagues the night before. She'd had enough of feeling inferior when in the company of his colleagues. She resolved to have it out with him when they arrived home.

This business trip, combined with partners socialising, was supposed to be a great weekend to relax together. Instead of taking the Eurostar to Paris, along with the others, they'd decided to drive across from Dover to Calais and then on to the south of Paris where the conference was being held. Jane did most of the driving so Andrew could concentrate on his presentation. On this return journey, she had to drive as he was still intoxicated from his excessive drinking last night. He'd spent the time complaining about not getting the train and missing the company of his colleagues.

Jane heard a scream and thud at the same time. Looking across, she saw Andrew flying through the air as a truck screeched to a stop. Her stomach heaved more. After vomiting, she staggered to where the truck driver had stopped with his hazard lights on. He'd left his cab and was looking at Andrew laying still on the hard shoulder. He said something to her in French which she didn't understand.

'It's my husband. We are English. Sorry, I don't speak French.'

'Dead. Sorry. No stopping.' The driver gesticulated with his hands as he spoke, then shrugged his shoulders in an apologetic way.

'He just got out of the car when I stopped. I felt unwell. He must've forgotten we're in France and walked into the road. I'm sorry this happened to you.'

'No. Me sorry. I phone police.'

The truck driver telephoned the police, then an ambulance arrived and all sorts of formalities ensued.

A motorist had pulled up soon after the accident and the driver offered assistance to Jane.

'I don't speak French. Would you be able to help me understand what's being said by the driver and the other people involved?'

'I'll gladly help if I can. A tragedy for you, returning home after a holiday?'

'Just a business conference and yes, a tragedy.'

Feeling frightened and alone, she suddenly realised that when this was sorted out, she'd be out of her abusive marriage and able to live her life.

For now though, she was the grieving widow with a mountain of formalities to deal with.

Too Trusting

I now know how easy it is to get fooled by someone.

'Trusting souls shouldn't be let out of the house,' my Gran used to say.

Fiona Biggs was known to be dishonest and came from a family of crooks. She was in tears when she called at our house and asked for a loan to visit her terminally ill mother in hospital. I asked her why she couldn't get the money from her father. She told me he was in jail and no use to anyone in their family. He was arrested for money laundering and drug dealing.

'What about friends?'

'How do people like us have friends? Everyone's on the take and just out for themselves.'

I didn't have the gumption to suggest that is exactly what she was like.

I told her I'd help her out but I would only have the money after lunch. I prepared an IOU for her to sign when she called in the afternoon. I wasn't going to give money to her so readily without proof of what I was owed.

While out shopping, I stopped to get the cash out of the cashpoint. As I was taking the money from the slot, I felt a person close to me.

Turning my head sideways, I saw it was Fiona. In a split second she had grabbed the cash and run off.

I shouted after her but that was no use. She was gone. I was really angry as she'd taken double what I was going to give her.

I headed straight for the police station where I eventually had an interview with a police woman. She was surprised that I'd been taken in by a known thief. CCTV would prove my story and she would eventually be apprehended for the crime.

The one thing she was honest about was her mother's illness. At her funeral, Fiona was arrested.

The Victim

I tried to help her. She constantly got herself into tight spots.

First it was spending on her credit cards when she started work. Young people shouldn't be allowed to have them. It took a year or two to sort that out.

The speeding fines followed. She should've been a racing driver. Then she lost her licence.

Drinking followed. A mouthy lot she ended up in company with. I suspected a bit of drug taking got mixed in with that.

Talking to her was no use.

Now she lies here, fighting for her life.

The victim of a stabbing.

Worse Than The Crime

This slow development would've put anyone to sleep.

She hadn't wanted to attend this meeting in the first place. All the groundwork to the crime was explained in extreme detail.

Why can't they just get going and explain what they'd found, what'd been examined, who'd been interviewed and what'd been decided from statements received? She felt someone was looking at her. Coming out of her reverie, she realised the chief had asked her a question.

'Sorry, Sir, could you repeat that?'

'It would seem that your thoughts are not with us today. Heavy night last night?'

'To be honest, Sir, I was considering suggesting that the first witness be questioned again. He seemed to have more knowledge about the incident than anyone else. How did he know exactly where the knife had entered the victim's body if he hadn't been in the same room? How did he know it was a knife and not another weapon, although that could've been an assumption? Other witnesses are uncertain of the exact whereabouts of each other in the building at the time. He could've committed the murder, discarded the knife in the waste bin, gone to the bathroom across the corridor, cleaned any blood traces from his clothing or body and been back in his office before anyone realised he'd been absent. We know gloves were used. Where are they? After all this time, they'll have been disposed of so no definite evidence there. We need to examine what he's to gain from the death of the victim, besides taking up his position in the company.'

'You've wriggled out of that one very well, Constable. We can't assume guilt where there is no evidence to back it up. Gut instincts went out of the window years ago. However, the point made of who'd gain from the victim's demise is valid and is the task I was appointing you with when you were in dreamland.'

She was fuming. Such inappropriate innuendos could not continue. Just because she had refused his advances. His attitude was worse than the crime they were investigating in her opinion. She determined to help solve this case, then bring him to book. And she had witnesses to his comments.

Braking Hard

He thanked all his friends for their support after his loss.

No-one knew what had actually happened. The garage had done a good repair job on the brakes, after he'd notified them that they were faulty.

The car in front stopped suddenly. Doris braked hard. The airbag had inflated. She was crushed between it and the back of her seat. A truck rammed into her from the back, shunting her into the car in front. She died immediately.

The compensation he received from the truck company would keep him comfortably off. He looked forward to enjoying unhindered golfing holidays.

Exercise Is Not For The Faint Hearted

All this activity left her with a splitting headache. She was determined to get fit and trim up for her wedding in a month's time. Just drink more water.

People were leaving the gym and she was just about to give up and go home herself, when she heard the weights on some equipment slam down, then a scream.

She ran over to the pull-down equipment and saw a small man hanging from the handle which had caught in his T-shirt; his left arm was dangling limply at his side. An instructor was trying to get him down but each time the weights were pulled, it tightened the shirt around his neck. Someone came running with a ladder. The instructor climbed up it to support the man, while his colleague managed to release the weights.

The little man fainted.

The instructor supporting him had a struggle to remain balanced on the ladder. A first aider had managed to drag an exercise mat to the area. They fell onto it. The ladder clattered on top of them.

She couldn't believe this was happening. How on earth had that man got himself into that situation? He must've been trying some stupid heroics.

There was suddenly a screech followed by high pitched laughter. The little man was hysterical, having successfully got everyone's attention when usually he felt he was invisible.

The manager of the gym arrived and led the little man away. As she left the gym, she noted that a policeman was in a meeting with the manager and the man. No doubt there would be repercussions on health and safety grounds as well as expulsion from the gym.

The Diamond Ring

Inspector Ball was contemplating his next case which looked like a done deal. A lad had been seen stealing a purse from an old lady's shopping bag.

She was frail looking and had stopped on the main street near the old well to rest. She was holding her bag by one handle. It gaped and showed the purse lying inside. It was a huge temptation. The lad couldn't resist the easy pickings.

When he dashed around the corner to count the cash, he found a diamond ring amongst the coins. What a bonus. He decided to take the ring to Billy the Dosh as he knew he would get loads for it.

Billy the Dosh recognised the ring as his grandmother's and had warned her about carrying it around in her purse. Angry with the lad for robbing his Granny, he thought he'd get on the good side of the law for a change. He took the lad to the police station with the ring.

However, the Inspector was not entirely convinced that the ring had been obtained for the 'Grandmother' by legitimate means. He investigated old burglaries where jewellery had been reported as stolen.

A fantastic result, two offenders apprehended and an old case closed.

Little Red Riding Hood By The Wolf

It was cold and I was very hungry. The little girl with the red hood called regularly to see her grandmother. The smell of food wafting from her basket was enticing.

I didn't want to frighten her but the only way of getting at that food was to pretend to be the grandmother. The last time Red Riding Hood left her grandmother, she didn't lock the door properly, so I crept in and laid in wait until the next day.

The grandmother was propped up in bed and when I raised my head to see if she was asleep, she saw me and started yelling. I went towards her and she stumbled away out of bed towards the bathroom. I followed her and as she fell, I tied her up, took her bonnet off and leapt into the bed before Red Riding Hood arrived. I didn't mean the old lady any harm but I did want the food.

It was a pity that Red Riding Hood couldn't understand that and was very frightened at seeing my hairy arms. I hadn't really eaten her grandmother. I only wanted Red Riding Hood to drop the food so I could eat it and stay warm and cosy for a short time.

Red Riding Hood dropped the basket of food and ran out of the cottage, screaming.

I jumped out of bed, stripped off grandmother's clothes, grabbed the food and ran into the woods. I could hear a rumpus as villagers were running with their guns. I was much quicker than them. I went into my dray and can stay there for days before surfacing for more food.

Poor grandmother.

A Crook With Morals

Just as he spotted the car hurtling down the road towards him, he jumped out of the way. It mounted the pavement and crashed into a wall.

The noise attracted a few people's attention. Scott noticed that Tyler was still alive. A man across the road was calling for an ambulance. Scott turned and walked away.

Tyler had said he would pay him back for refusing that last job.

There was no way he was going to rob a defenceless old woman in her own home. Selling drugs to idiots was one thing. He would not partake of violence.

Nightmares

'Where is she? I'll have her head on the block when I find her.'

The words kept ringing through her head. Vicky knew his bark was worse than his bite, especially at the end of a stressful day. She knew she was at fault for not putting the medical equipment in the steriliser before being called urgently to tend to another patient at the clinic. No other patients were due for treatment in the surgery.

She was trying to run down the corridor but her legs felt like lead. She arrived at the surgery. No one was there. She went to the dirty instrument tray to pick it up and put the contents into the steriliser.

Looking down, she saw blood on the floor seeping from behind the trolley. A head lay behind the trolley, a face just like hers looking up at her. She screamed.

The loud noise woke her up. Her daughter had slammed the door open and was next to her in the bedroom.

'Mum, are you ok?'

'Yes, just that dream again. I'll go and shower.'

'It's your day off - long weekend. Don't you remember? We're going into the hills for some fresh air.'

Vicky sank back onto her pillow. She was so relieved to have time to recover. She couldn't understand why she kept having that same nightmare.

The day out with Rose was brilliant. While walking, Rose suggested to her that she make an appointment to see the GP.

'He could maybe recommend counselling to find out what the underlying worry is that is making you have those dreams.'

'You do have faith in talking things through. I'll be asked all sorts of strange things and it will still happen.'

'Please do this, Mum, just for me. We lose too much sleep over it.' Rose had noticed how anxious her mother had become over the past few months and jumped at the slightest noise; how she didn't seem to be able to finish her meals and was losing weight. Rose knew that her mother's boss was to blame for making her life such a misery and now lack of sleep was being added.

Vicky duly made the appointment with the GP, who did as Rose had predicted and set up a meeting with a counsellor.

As Vicky guessed, she was asked umpteen questions she thought were really irrelevant. She answered them all honestly.

The strangest thing happened when the counsellor asked her about her taste in films. Vicky told her that she enjoyed old films, the black and white ones mainly. She suddenly recalled that she stopped watching a film which she thought was ridiculous because the actor looked like her surgeon boss and the nurse had a slight resemblance to herself. On that occasion, she'd told Rose about the film. Rose was curious about it and watched it while her mother was preparing their supper. When Vicky walked into the room to tell Rose their supper was ready, she saw the head of the nurse on the floor. It seems the surgeon had overbalanced while performing the operation. His arm had swung out to try to regain his balance. The nurse was standing on the right side of him at the patient's head. The scalpel had caught her in the neck and they both fell. The added weight of the fall hadn't totally severed the head, although it looked like it in the age-blurred film.

While the film was rather far-fetched, that image had played on Vicky's mind for some time. She thought she'd overcome her initial reaction to it.

The counsellor asked if they'd watched the film to the end. Vicky recalled that Rose had turned it off straight away, seeing the distress it caused her mother. They hadn't talked about it since. Vicky didn't even know what the film was called.

The counsellor suggested that she talk to Rose about it at home. Rose remembered the film. She told Vicky she'd managed to watch it again on another occasion. The nurse's head wasn't cut off. She had a bad gash which looked worse in black and white and also due to the film being out of focus.

Rose had been very worried about her mother's mental state and had mentioned it to her boyfriend on several occasions when they met. She also mentioned the film to him. He said it sounded like a great way for the consultant to go, in the theatre where he put the frighteners on everyone. Rose said she thought that would be awful for anyone working there as they are life savers, not life takers. He agreed that it would be horrible and his remark was only a sick joke.

Two weeks later, when Vicky went to see the counsellor on her day off, she mentioned what Rose had told her about the film. At that point, the nightmare hadn't recurred. The counsellor agreed that the conflict of fact and fiction had played havoc with Vicky's subconscious thoughts.

The following day, when Vicky arrived at the clinic, she was surprised at how many police vehicles were in the car park.

'What's happened?' she asked Marion at the reception desk.

'Mr Saunders was found dead in the theatre ante-room this morning by the cleaner. He must've been there all night.'

'That's awful. How did he die?'

'Not sure yet but there's been a whisper of murder by stabbing. He was in his street clothes. Plenty of people have been upset by his temper. It's a wonder you worked with him for so long without snapping. No surgery today.'

Vicky was shaken, almost as if that film had actually happened.

'I need a cuppa. I'll be in the canteen if anyone asks. After that I'll report to Sister.'

She definitely hoped that nightmare wouldn't recur.

When Vicky arrived home, she told Rose the consultant had been found dead.

'You didn't find him, did you?' Rose didn't want her mother having awful nightmares again. Vicky shook her head.

'No, it was one of the cleaners who come in very early. She was so shocked she had to have counselling before being sent home.'

'Poor woman.' Rose's sympathies were with the cleaning lady. Vicky was surprised that Rose didn't seem overly concerned about the consultant's death.

'I'm relieved for your sake, Mum and for the other staff who he's mentally abused over the years. Whoever did it, did everyone a favour.'

'It wasn't only the staff. He's been rude to patients and their families as well. The police are going to have a job on to solve this one.'

'Well, you weren't there yesterday, so you're in the clear,' Rose said, smiling at her mother.

Later when she was alone, Rose recalled the conversation she'd had with her boyfriend previously regarding the film which bothered her mother. She wondered whether her boyfriend had anything to do with it. Some of his friends were a bit shady, but surely? Whatever, Rose was content in the knowledge that someone had managed to do the deed. There'd be no more verbal abuse for her mum at work.

Well Earned Rest

It had begun to get on her nerves. Television, day in and day out. Some fun in him being retired.

'Can't you find a hobby that will interest you?'

'Like what, smart ass? You make so many suggestions about what I should do. Why don't you do something useful instead of going to lunch with your mates all the time?'

'Once a month with the girls from work and knitting once a fortnight certainly isn't all the time. I spend more time cleaning and tidying up after you. You don't bother to help. You could take an interest in the garden at least.'

'You know I've got a bad back and can't do heavy jobs. Cleaning is too much for me, gardening is even worse.' Sarah could have thrown something at him. She'd seen him reaching up in the wardrobe for a heavy box last week and there wasn't any sign of a groan from him. He had been startled when she saw him. He said it was just some paperwork he was putting away.

'That's why I said get a hobby. You could go to the library and research your family tree. That wouldn't be onerous, would it? Maybe find some long-lost family members and become more sociable.'

'What's wrong with me just resting and enjoying my well-earned retirement. You've had plenty of years just sitting around on the money I've earned.'

'If that's the way you look at housework, shopping, gardening and keeping to a tight budget, maybe I should take a well-earned rest myself.'

With that, she left the house to do the shopping. She also had a walk around the park, prolonging her time out in the fresh air.

When she returned home, Thomas was nowhere to be found in the house. She decided to look in that box in his wardrobe. Taking the ladders upstairs, after double-locking the doors in the house, she found his stash of pornographic horrors. She was sickened to the core. How had she ever missed that coming into the house? No wonder he didn't want her to go into his wardrobe.

She left them where she had found them and went downstairs, thinking hard. She'd forgotten she had double-locked the doors and was roused out of her thoughts by him banging on the front door.

'Why have you locked me out? Who've you got in there?'

'I must've put the catch down accidentally when I came in. No one's in here. No one likes coming here anymore with your boorish attitude. What've you bought today?' She noticed the bag he was carrying.

'Nothing that you'd be interested in, just something for my enjoyment.'

She decided that she wasn't going to be fobbed off and grabbed at the bag. It ripped and several magazines and a DVD fell out. He lunged for them but she'd grabbed them first.

'What filth have you brought into this house? It belongs in the bin.'

'Give them to me, they're not yours.' As he went to grab them from her, she shoved him out of her way and ran to the back door, forgetting she'd double-locked it. While she was fumbling to open it, shouting at him that they certainly weren't hers, he lunged at her grabbing her hand away from the door. She flung her free arm out and hit him with the magazines, catching him in his eyes. He fell over, hitting his head on the corner of the table.

'Oh, my God, what've I done?' At first he lay motionless on the floor and then started to groan. She was relieved that he wasn't dead. She didn't touch him.

'What's happened? Why am I lying on the floor?'

'Don't you remember that you slipped on your magazines after I threw them at you?'

He still lay there, looking at her, touching his head where a lump was forming. 'No, help me get up.'

'Can't you try to get up on your own?'

'I think my back is hurt.'

'Shall I call an ambulance then?'

'No, help me up.' As she went to put her arms under his, he used his strength to pull her onto the floor. He rolled over onto her and pinned her arms above her head. 'You bitch. You'd kill me, would you? Over some harmless magazines? I'll show you whose boss.'

As he released one of his arms to hit her across the face, she managed to slip from under his grasp and rolled away. Getting up quicker than him, she realised that he'd slumped back onto the floor, face down and groaning about his back.

'I'm phoning for an ambulance.' She left him lying there in agony and called the emergency number.

'They'll be here as soon as they can.' He stayed on the floor, groaning.

She decided not to move the magazines where they lay near his feet on the floor. That would give authenticity to her story.

When the ambulance crew arrived, they looked around at the neat kitchen. The magazines and the man were the only objects out of place.

Sarah introduced herself and her husband, Thomas.

'Well, how'd you manage to get yourself in this position, Thomas?' Without waiting for an answer, they established where he was hurting and asked if he'd a history of back problems. They managed to turn him over.

Sarah explained that he was taking the magazines out to the bin when he'd dropped them as he was going to unlock the door, then slipped on them as he'd stepped back. She wasn't sure if they believed her. It was the best she could do to protect herself.

Once they'd examined his legs and established how badly he was injured, they decided to take him to hospital. After they'd managed to get Thomas onto the stretcher and out of the house, they told Sarah which hospital they would be taking him to. It was further than their local one but Sarah could drive so would follow on with his essential items.

Leaving the magazines in the kitchen, she went to their bedroom taking the ladder with her. She took all the magazines out of the box and put them in the recycling bin. All the DVDs and other ugly items in the box were going to be parcelled up and taken to the tip the next day. If Thomas ever came home again, things would be very different.

At the hospital, Sarah found out that Thomas had injuries which would probably leave him permanently disabled. Time would tell.

In the meantime, she had peace and a well-earned rest to look forward to at home.

Helping The Family

Talking about life was easy for Uncle Jim. He'd learnt his lesson well, having served time in prison for burglary. He'd got in with a bad lot, did it for a laugh and then regretted it when the people being robbed got hurt.

Since his release, he'd led a good life but never married. His only problem was that he loved his pint and could ramble on about anything when in his cups.

Mum had been ill for some time and now she was in hospital for treatment. Uncle Jim had offered to come and care for us, supervising the morning school runs and our evening chores. Cooking the meals was a bit hit and miss but we didn't starve.

I don't know what made him go on about how it's best not to get in with a bad lot one particular evening. It made me feel really guilty but I hoped I kept an innocent look on my face.

Mum didn't even know that I'd been making parcel deliveries for 'Mr Big'. When Mum lost her job because of her illness, we were sometimes short of money. I took to asking around about odd jobs after school. One man told me that if I could be trusted, his boss could maybe use my services from time to time.

'What does it involve?' I asked. 'I have to go to school and have to help my Mum around the house in the evenings.' This chap called himself Tommy.

'No surnames need be used,' he'd said.

He told me to meet him at a corner near the market the following afternoon so he could tell me what the job would involve.

The next day I met him straight after school.

'I've spoken to my boss. Call him Mr Big. He isn't a big man, just a big presence in the town.'

I'd never heard of him but then I was only a teenage kid with responsibilities at home.

'We need someone to pick up and deliver parcels. You'll only find out where the pick-up and drop off will be when the job demands it.'

'What's in the parcels?'

'Ask no questions, be told no lies,' he replied. That amazed me, a saying of my Gran's, God bless her. We did miss her.

At first, I was a bit apprehensive but the parcels were small, light and fitted into my rucksack. The drop-offs were at odd places and I had to make sure that no one was around when I completed my tasks. I received cash the day after the drop at a pre-arranged place, avoiding using the same meeting place. All a bit cloak and dagger but I didn't worry, so long as I could help Mum out.

'Phil, how do you manage to bring home so much food with the money I give you for the shopping?' she had asked one day.

'There were special offers late on when vegetables and some meat at market stalls had been reduced.' I had answered confidently to allay her suspicions. After that I was careful about what I spent and brought home, just slipping some treats in now and again.

'I don't want to do this forever, Tommy, just until Mum is well again. Also, only once or twice a week,' I told him, the next time I saw him. That seemed to suit him.

Then, after Mum had been taken into hospital, I was asked to do three jobs. One was to a new place and I was worried about the area but followed the instructions to the letter. I was a bit later getting home.

'Where've you been? It's getting late now?' Uncle Jim was worried.

'Been larking about with some of the lads. Sorry, I forgot the time. It won't happen again.'

The next day I met Tommy for my payment.

'What'd you do with the delivery? It didn't arrive at the correct place.'

I told him exactly where I had dropped it off, the colour of the door and who took it. 'Well, someone is lying but I believe you. I can't pay you because I have to find out who has the parcel.'

We arranged to meet the next day at a different rendezvous. When he arrived, he looked like he'd been in a fight.

'You ok, Tommy?'

'Yes. People are pinning the blame on you for the lost parcel. I've stuck up for you and ended up with a bloodied face. People are getting really angry about this parcel. Mr Big's asking to see you but I told him that was out of the question.'

Tommy was the only one who knew where I lived and I started to become a bit nervous about this whole thing.

'Maybe I shouldn't do any more work if stuff's going to go missing,' I said, really scared now.

'That'd make you look guilty. I'll be in touch.'

That night, I was left downstairs doing my homework while Uncle Jim went to bed. My two brothers were upstairs in their bedroom at the back of the house. Mine was the smaller bedroom at the front, next to Mum's where Uncle Jim was sleeping.

Suddenly I heard a car race up and screech to a halt. Someone tapped at the door but I wouldn't answer. I panicked and ducked down behind the settee. The doors were double-locked and no one could get in. There was a gunshot at the same time as the window pane shattered into the room. Then a car door slammed and the car screeched away. I was trembling but needed to make sure my brothers were alright. I quietly went up the stairs but there were no sounds except for Uncle Jim's snoring. I wondered if I should wake him and while hesitating I saw blue lights flashing through the window above the front door. I knew I had to wake him and the whole sorry tale would come out.

The police knocked at the door as I was shaking Uncle Jim. He roused himself and I went downstairs.

'Who is it?' I asked through the door.

'The police. We need to come in.' I unlocked the door and peered through the slit with the security chain in place.

'Open the door properly and let the officers in, lad,' Uncle Jim said as he came down the stairs.

The policemen came in and looked at the damage the shot had made of the window and the room. Uncle Jim looked at me but said nothing.

'Why would anyone want to do this kind of damage?' I was shaking so much from the shock of all this, I couldn't have put two words together. I didn't want to drop anyone in it either. If this is what happened after a missing parcel, it would be worse if I told on them.

'I was only doing my homework. I heard a car but didn't look out to see what it was like or who was in it or anything.' I managed to stammer.

'The couple next door had woken with the noise and saw the car driving off. They didn't get its number. They could only tell that it looked like a black BMW. They reported the disturbance to us.'

'Do either of you know anyone who drives a black BMW?'

'No, I don't.' We both answered in unison. I could be totally honest and truthful about that.

They gave us the number of a firm who'd come out to board up the window for the night and also gave us their emergency number on a card before they left.

'If you can think of anyone who could be responsible for this, please contact us.'

When they'd left, Uncle Jim phoned the repairers.

'What do you know about this, Phil?' We were waiting for the repair men to arrive. I poured it all out to him then. I'd only been trying to help the family. I was also insistent on telling him I'd not had anything to do with the missing parcel apart from deliver it to the drop-off as instructed.

'Leave it all to me.'

'Please don't get yourself hurt, or get in with these men yourself. You've been going straight for so many years.'

'Don't worry, lad, I'm not about to go down that road again.'

Two nights later, after my brothers had gone to bed, Uncle Jim had a little chat with me.

'I know who Mr Big is but I'm not going to tell you. I've information about Mr Big that could put him in jail. I've told Mr Big to take his heavies off you and leave you alone for the rest of your life. I told him you're an honest lad and shouldn't have got caught up in this business at all. I also told him that you'd not told the police anything as you were so scared by the blast you couldn't speak. Mr Big and his gang won't be coming near you again.'

'What about Tommy? Is he alright?'

'You don't have to worry about him at all. He had a bit of a beating but he'll get over it. Don't waste your sympathies on him. He's leading the life he chose. You've a better future ahead of you so long as you stay away from trouble and concentrate on your schoolwork.'

'Mum'll be really mad when she hears of this.'

'Well, we won't tell her any lies but we needn't tell her everything as she'll worry too much. She'll need to be stress free while she recovers when she gets home and we'll see that she is. You should've come to me when you realised that things were so tight for your Mum. Promise me that's what you'll do in the future.'

We shook hands on that, although I would've loved to hug him for his understanding and help to sort this horror out.

Uncle Jim stopped his drinking while staying with us and relaxed more around us. It was so great to have Mum home after a short while. She was relieved that the damage caused had been repaired and everything was cleaned up after the forensics team had inspected everything and taken a bullet away. She wouldn't have liked to see the mess from the broken window.

'And all a case of a mistaken property,' she said, quoting a newspaper.

That's when I realised that there are two roads named Regent but one was a street and one was a road. Looking at Uncle Jim, he must've realised by my face what I thought but he smiled and winked at me. No more was ever said again.

The Attack

DI Philimore drove his car to the end of the alley.

'What the hell?' He slammed on brakes to avoid hitting the woman who fell off the pavement.

'I'll go.' His sergeant jumped out of the car.

The woman was struggling to get up and the sergeant urged her to sit on the pavement.

'How badly are you hurt?'

'It's not from the fall, lad. I've been battered and was trying to get away from him. He's back there but could've seen you and skedaddled.'

The sergeant looked around. By now DI Philimore had left the car and heard the last comment the woman made.

He asked quickly, 'What does he look like? What's he wearing? What's his name?' He was thinking of the call that had been made reporting a disturbance in the area.

'Tall, ginger hair. Donkey jacket. Calls himself Tiny.'

'See if you can find him, Sarge. Now, Madam, do you think I can help you up?'

They walked back to her home, while she told him the story.

139

'My son, James, got in with a bad lot. He was driving for them when they were doing drug runs, robbing premises where users didn't pay up and also driving the thugs who beat up dealers who didn't pass on the payments. He was caught after a 'sting' and is now serving time inside. The gang say he stashed some money away. If he did, I don't know where it is. He didn't live here. They keep coming here and hounding me. Today I told Tiny I'm going to call the police if I see any of them near me again. That's when he turned nasty, started tearing my house to bits and when I started screaming and running for my door, he attacked me. Mrs Walker next door banged on the wall and then came round to the front door to see if I was ok. He wouldn't let her in but I ran out the back while he was barring her way.'

By this time, they had reached the terraced house. The inspector asked her what her name was.

'Susan Jackson. You may know my son as JJ. I was once visited by the police when he was being investigated but they didn't bother me after that.' The front room was a bit of a mess, with cupboard doors open and contents strewn around.

The DI introduced himself and said the sergeant was Joe Bailey.

'Do you want to make a formal complaint against Tiny for assault?'

'Oh, no, Sir. Others will come back and make my life hell.'

'Well, can you help us with our enquiries? Can we send our forensics team in? That may help us to identify Tiny and the gang he's with.'

Susan agreed to that, so long as they didn't take too long. She sat down wearily on a kitchen chair. The Inspector asked if she needed to phone for a doctor. She said not but he insisted that she have someone with her and also that she didn't touch anything else in the room.

There was a knock at the door. The woman was looking concerned and asked if Susan was alright. She said she was Mrs Walker from next door and had made the call to the police. Susan called her to come into the kitchen while the Inspector, still standing at the door, called the station. Sergeant Bailey came panting up the road and leaning against the outside wall said he hadn't been able to find any trace of Tiny, although some people had told him in which direction the man had run. The Inspector asked the sergeant to stay with the women until the forensics team arrived, while he went back to the station.

Susan made the sergeant a drink of tea. He asked if there was any other room Tiny had been in and when she said no, he decided to leave the women to themselves and stand outside.

The Inspector had a short walk back to his car, noticing twitching curtains at some of the windows. He was thoughtful as he drove back to the station, trying to remember details of the case. He immediately went to see his colleague, DI Stella Mayfield, who had been in charge of the James Jackson case.

'Hi Stella, have you got a minute or two to spare?'

'For you, Phil, all the time in the world. What can I help you with?' They had worked together for many years and knew how each other operated in their separate teams, having a great respect for each other's ethos.

Phil told Stella of the morning's events, how they had received the call about a disturbance at a property in the Butterfield district and the victim being James Jackson's mother. He asked her to briefly update him on the background to the case.

'We had been watching the Brownley gang for a while but had no solid evidence to arrest any of the team. Preferably we wanted to get all of them in one go. We had an officer undercover in the area on the night we arrested JJ. A big delivery of cocaine was expected at the old warehouses on Station Road. When it was made, we pounced but some of the gang managed to get away across fields. We only caught JJ in a car chase as he took the leader, Barry Costain and two other accomplices away from the scene on back roads. Of course, they all pleaded not guilty but with traces of cocaine on their clothing, apart from JJ who had remained in the car, they were prosecuted and imprisoned. JJ's sentence is the lightest. He's due out in another three months' time. All four of them were sent to different prisons and contacts are being monitored as we believe there's still activity going on with other gang members. Tiny fits the profile of reports from assault victims who won't risk laying a charge against him. I'm sure the forensic results will throw up a positive identity. JJ wasn't very forthcoming with information but now that his mother's been attacked, he may think differently. Shall we visit him together to see what his reaction is and if we can, encourage him to be more co-operative?'

Phil agreed to that and left Stella to make arrangements with the prison. He went to his office to file his report and check up with the sergeant at the house to see how things were progressing.

The forensics team had arrived and were busy taking samples in the living room and from the front door. A lad had come with a mug to borrow some sugar. When the sergeant had shown the lad into the kitchen, Mrs Jackson had given him the powder form of a sweetener branded with the name 'Contact', out of a box she had in her kitchen cupboard. The sergeant had asked her if she uses it but she said she prefers normal sugar to that slimming stuff.

'Anyway, I tried a spoon of it one night in my tea and couldn't sleep. I cleaned my house from top to bottom before finally going to bed, exhausted and felt bad the next day. I could only blame it on that slimming stuff, so don't use it at all. James gave it to me to keep for him in case he needed it when he was here, or in case young Neil's family ran out as they only use that 'Contact' stuff.'

Alarm bells rang when the sergeant relayed this conversation to the DI. He instructed the sergeant to get the forensics team to examine the 'Contact'.

Susan was surprised when the men in white wanted to look at the slimming stuff. She had a few boxes of it that James had left there, so showed it all to them. They asked her if she really thought it was 'Contact', as the boxes had been opened and re-sealed. She said that's what James had told her, although he did tell her not to use it herself if she ran out of sugar. Mrs Walker was amazed at all that was going on and sat open-mouthed wondering what was coming next.

After examining the open packet and one of the re-sealed ones, the forensics team told Susan they were taking it away with them. She asked why and wondered what young Neil's family were going to say. When the team told her that it wasn't 'Contact' but was in fact cocaine and worth thousands of pounds on the streets, she was visibly shaken and almost fainted. How could her own son deceive her like this?

The sergeant got on the phone to DI Philimore to let him know the latest developments.

'Don't move from your post, Sergeant. I'm coming back with a search warrant. Don't let Mrs Jackson go into any of the rooms either. We'll inform the forensics team to stay put as well, for now.' The sergeant wondered what was going on, as he had no idea what Mrs Jackson's son had been up to. Orders are orders, so he stayed put.

DI Philimore contacted DI Mayfield.

'You're not going to believe this. It seems young James Jackson does have something to hide after all.'

After DI Philimore had finished relaying the events at the house, DI Mayfield said she'd get the search warrant sorted out and accompany him back to the house, along with a couple of officers from her team.

When they arrived at the house, they found Mrs Jackson in a distressed state. Mrs Walker was trying to calm her down as best she could. What an awful day this was turning out to be and how much worse was it going to get? Her face, arms and legs were beginning to ache where Tiny had beaten her.

'We need to search your house to see if James hid anything else here, Mrs Jackson. This is the search warrant. We'll try to be as tidy as we can but if there's anything else you know of that he left here for safe keeping, can you let us know?' There were occasions when DI Philimore didn't like his job much and this was one of them. However, if they could rid the house of anything that would bring the thugs back to bully Mrs Jackson, it was worthwhile.

Mrs Jackson told them that James sometimes used the spare bedroom at the back. He also had a couple of boxes stored in the attic. She herself lived in the front bedroom and understood that they should look through her things as well, in case he had put something in there without her knowing it. Susan became quite upset when she mentioned that she didn't want her husband's ashes disturbing. They were in the copper pot on her dressing table.

Mrs Walker hugged her friend and asked if she could take her to her house while the police were doing their search. Both DIs thought it'd be less stressful for Mrs Jackson and consented. The women left through the back door as a little crowd had gathered round the front out of curiosity.

One young lad asked the sergeant, 'There been someone killed, copper?'

'No, thank goodness,' replied the sergeant. 'Now run along and go home. There's no need for you to be here, or anyone else for that matter,' addressing the rest of the group as he looked around at all of them. He noticed a short distance away at the other side of the street, a ginger-haired big bulky person wearing a donkey jacket. He couldn't go after the lad he believed to be Tiny himself but spoke to control over his radio and asked for help to apprehend the man.

DI Philimore came out of the house to update the sergeant on what had been discovered regarding JJ, which had resulted in the drug squad being involved. The sergeant mentioned to the DI that he had asked for help to arrest the man standing across the street. The DI looked in that direction just as an unmarked police car pulled up and three plain clothes policemen took hold of the man. He tried to push them out the way to run but they were prepared and knocked him to the ground before handcuffing him and bundling him into the back seat. Sergeant Bailey was praised for his quick thinking.

Inside the house, the forensics team examined the ashes in the copper pot and were relieved to find there was nothing sinister in it. The rest of Mrs Jackson's bedroom contained nothing out of the ordinary either. The boxes in the attic were examined. Most contained childhood items, old books and photographs. Under some soft toys in one box was a large plastic sleeve containing a bundle of bank notes. This must have been what Tiny was after. A small packet of cocaine was found in the spare bedroom amongst some clothing presumed to belong to JJ.

It took around three hours to search the small house. After forensics had left, both DIs knocked on the neighbour's door and asked to speak to Mrs Jackson alone. In the front room, they told Susan what they had found. DI Mayfield said she'd need to interview Susan officially at the police station but she'd no need to worry about that for now. They were both concerned for Susan's health and insisted that she see a doctor as soon as it could be arranged.

Susan told them that Mrs Walker had already taken that in hand. She had an appointment later on in the afternoon when her friend was going to accompany her as she didn't want to be out on her own.

'You can go back to your house now, Mrs Jackson. We've tried to be as neat as we could. Sergeant Bailey will stay a while if you need any help with moving heavy items. We've a few things to clear up at the station but will be in touch in the next few days. If you have any problems or think of anything that can be useful, please contact us.' DI Philimore handed both his and DI Mayfield's cards to Susan.

Susan went back to her house with Sergeant Bailey who helped her put bulky items where they belonged, then left.

When DI Philimore and DI Mayfield visited JJ in prison the next day, he decided to confess everything he knew. He never believed that his mother would be 'done over'. His co-operation would be unlikely to reduce a new sentence imposed for his active part in drug dealing.

Injustice

Life without Anton had become bearable but only just. I missed his greeting when I arrived home, our daily walks, talking through the problems of the day with him listening intently, head to one side. The snuggles on the settee in the evening watching a movie together.

The woman's screams still rang in my head. Anton had broken free from me to jump on her attacker. He had been shot then bludgeoned to death with the butt of the gun.

The woman's gratitude was overwhelming.

The police awarded Anton posthumously for canine bravery.

The attacker received a custodial sentence.

Smuggling

The Russians were feeling satisfied, having successfully sent their packages abroad.

The World Cup Football Tournament had been successful. The couriers of the deadly poison had mingled with the supporters. Undercover agents melted into the crowds. The couriers passed Russian dolls, containing hidden phials, to unsuspecting visitors as they left their hotels for the airports.

The shot of fluorescent dye on their jackets would be noticeable to the agents when they arrived at their destinations. The 'imposter' dolls would be swopped for genuine ones.

All was prepared in twelve countries for the elimination of the enemies of the State.

The Stabbing

Bob was relating what he had heard. Peggy interrupted that he couldn't be right. Garth tried to show the photo on his phone. Jim played back the video he had recorded.

'There's a certain amount of confusion here about what actually happened. First of all, I want to know exactly where each one of you was when the victim was being chased. One at a time please.' Sergeant Murray shouted to make himself heard.

Sirens were sounding and blue lights flashing as more police and an ambulance arrived at the scene.

Bob said he was just coming out of the chemist as the man raced passed. Peggy said she was in the café across the street, staring out of the window. Garth was standing at the bus stop. Jim happened to be taking a video on his phone of the window display at the estate agents and turned around as the man rushed passed. As each person said their piece, Sergeant Murray looked around the area to confirm their positions in relation to the incident.

'Can I see the recording? I'll also need to take your phone to get the video downloaded as it's important evidence.' Sergeant Murray was impressed.

'You not only captured the man who was running but also the person who was chasing him and the subsequent events.'

'The victim is the son of the Casino owner.' someone shouted from the crowd. No one had seen the man who chased him before.

They had all seen the victim being stabbed in the back and fall to the ground, the attacker kick him, then run off as they shouted. He must've been covered with blood from the injuries he had inflicted on his victim.

At the police station, when Sergeant Murray obtained the copy of the video, he showed it to his colleagues. Sergeant Kemp recognised the suspect as a person he'd apprehended a few years ago. He thought about the crime that'd been committed on that occasion, which had been an assault. The person's name was Cliff Ward, who'd been imprisoned for his crime. They searched their online records and found that he'd been released about eighteen months previously. It seems he'd been keeping a low profile since then.

A call was put out for his arrest, stating where he'd last been seen.

An officer had accompanied the victim, Brian Rogers, to the hospital and reported that although he was in a bad way, his injuries were not life threatening.

Of course, there was media interest and a lot of speculation which one of the clerks, Julie, was detailed to monitor in case any interesting facts were revealed about either of the men and their backgrounds.

When the casino owner, Sean Rogers was interviewed, he revealed that he had employed Cliff Ward as a security officer over fifteen months ago.

'He seems to be honest in his dealings with people and has never caused any bother since he's been working here. I have no explanation as to why there's now a problem between my son and Cliff Ward.'

Julie reported that on social media, a woman named Mary had messaged another named Jane regarding the assault, asking if Cliff Ward was her 'fella'. A different post on Brian Rogers' page stated that Jane was at his bedside 'comforting her boyfriend'.

Whilst this caused a little amusement, it was of great concern to the officers as they were aware this could lead to further repercussions. The sooner they arrested Cliff Ward, the better, to save him from a revenge attack.

All Cliff Ward's known haunts were visited and his known contacts were told to tell him to give himself up for his own safety. Later that night, he walked into the police station and handed himself in.

Under questioning, he revealed that there'd been some double crossing by Brian Rogers where gambling off the premises was concerned and the final straw was when he made a play for his girlfriend.

'The evidence against you is watertight as there's video footage of the incident. We are holding you at the station overnight for your own safety.'

Sergeant Murray left the interview room deep in thought. He would discuss Ward's allegations about the illegal gambling with the supervisor in the morning. For now, he'd a lot to write up about.

The following morning, the Supervisor suggested that they get more details from Ward about his allegations so they could look into it further. Possibly the vice squad already knew something about this. He'd arranged to have a meeting with Detective Bell about this case.

Detective Sydney Bell was pleased to be of assistance to his colleagues. They were aware of the underhand activities of Brian Rogers.

'We've been keeping an eye on him for a while. He first came to our attention when a young banker had been found with his hand in the till, literally. He was in debt up to his neck and was being violently threatened by an associate of Rogers. He's now in prison serving a short sentence but his credibility for a position of trust in the future has been ruined. We haven't been able to nail Rogers yet. We have two premises under surveillance, as well as his father's business. That appears to be legitimate.' Sydney consulted his files, then continued.

'One establishment is registered as a male boarding house. On appearance, all seems to be above board. We've had reports of men entering late at night and disappearing into the cellar. We are trying to get an undercover officer into the cellar but have so far failed. We're still working on it. It's that establishment where the young banker did his gambling, playing cards.

The other establishment is a social club, open during the day for the local people to use and in the evening various activities take place: dance classes, bingo, keep fit and the like. There's a room upstairs which is kept locked but on several nights a week the caretaker is instructed to leave the premises by Rogers, the registered owner of the building, by ten o'clock. Evidently, once the normal activities of the club shut down at ten p.m., an employee of Rogers takes charge of the entrance and who comes in. Those activities are a mystery. We have to tread carefully in our investigations.

This latest development may help us gain insight into Rogers' activities. As Ward is so tightly incriminated in the stabbing, he may be able to help us further. Is he willing to talk?' Detective Bell asked Sergeant Murray.

'We kept him in cells overnight. He's appearing in court this morning after which we're sure he'll be on remand pending his trial for assault and grievous bodily harm. Rogers' wound isn't life threatening. We could ask him what he knows. It's likely he'll be a marked man, anyway, when he's free to walk the streets.'

'For now, we'll leave it at that and we can discuss how to proceed once you've spoken to him.' Detective Bell ended the discussion.

Sergeant Murray arranged for Ward to be brought to an interview room to discuss the possibility of him helping the police with their enquiries. He was to be detained until his trial date. Ward was hesitant about telling them what he knew, as he'd be more vulnerable, even when he was serving a sentence in prison. He was assured he'd have as much protection as the force could give him. He said he'd like to think about it.

'Can we arrange a discussion with one of our detectives on a related case? It may help him from a different angle.' Sergeant Murray was not going to give up easily.

'I don't suppose there's much harm in that. I don't know what he wants to know until he asks me.'

'We'll arrange an interview with him for tomorrow morning. Thank you for your co-operation.'

Sergeant Murray left the interview room as Ward was taken back to his cell. He arranged with Detective Bell for the interview to take place the following afternoon.

Ward had decided to tell the officers all he knew, which turned out to be very little but enlightening in some ways.

Detective Bell started the questioning, after confirming that the interview was being recorded.

'What goes on in the cellar of the men's boarding house that is owned by Brian Rogers?'

'I've only been there once when I had to deliver a package from the boss to his son. I don't know what the package contained. The size indicated it was notes. I had to knock on the door, a spy hole was opened, then the door and I was allowed in. There's a little landing before the carpeted stairs lead down to a large cellar which is divided into two rooms, as far as I could tell. There's also a toilet as I saw the sign for it. There were gaming tables around the room. Roulette, cards and such like. At the time when I went, there weren't many people in. Brian took the package off me and asked his men to show me out again. That's all I know.'

'What about the upstairs room at the Social Club?'

Ward seemed hesitant about divulging his knowledge of that.

'Do you know what goes on there? Who goes there?' Detective Bell was getting impatient.

'That's heavy stuff. There are soft furnishings all around. There are small rooms off a large one. I only saw two doors open when I had to fetch a package from there for Mr Rogers senior. There was a bed in each and they looked clean. There seemed to be a proper bathroom on that floor as well. One room is used as an office and that's where I went. I noticed one closed door had a heavy lock on it.'

'Who was in the area?' the detective was getting a sense of more shenanigans than he had at first thought.

'Only Brian and his female assistant. She was introduced to me as Sally, that's all. She was well-dressed. Fitted in with the neatness of the place.'

'What time of day was it that you went there.'

'It was late afternoon. I was only there for a few minutes.'

'Is there anything else you can tell us? What about two women named Mary and Jane?'

'How'd you know about them?' Cliff was visibly shocked that the women had been mentioned.

'Their names came up in the process of our enquiries. Are they connected to the Casino in any way?'

'I may as well tell you all, as you'll find out eventually anyway. Mary is a friend of Jane, my girlfriend. Well, she's supposed to be my girl. Brian met her when she came to see me at work. He turned on the charm and she was impressed. I found out that he'd contacted her and arranged to meet her behind my back. That really bugged me. Then, on the day I chased him and stabbed him with the letter opener, he asked me to take a package to the boarding house. I felt the package was heavy and a different shape, so asked him if it was a gold bar. He said it was white gold. I refused to handle it as I'm not being a courier for drugs. He pulled out a small gun and was going to shoot me but I threw the package at him and was going to go for him, when he ran. I don't know why I picked up the letter opener and chased him. It's as if something snapped inside me. I'd vowed to myself to stay straight when I came out, then I did a stupid thing like that. I haven't seen Jane for over a week, so don't know what she's up to.'

Both officers were taken aback at the confession and details of the assault from Cliff.

'Where's the letter opener now?' Sergeant Murray needed that as evidence in the case.

'I chucked it in a bin somewhere along the way after I ran. I couldn't tell you where exactly as I was in a panic.'

'We'll do a search of the route, if you can tell us where you ended up?'

'I holed up in the park. There's a makeshift tent near a wall down by the river. Another rough sleeper gave me some food and brought the newspaper to show me the reports. I was cold and wanted clean clothes. I decided to hand myself in as I knew you would be watching my flat for me to appear.'

'You've given us quite a lot of information, Cliff. We don't know yet what charges will be brought against you. However, we'll bear in mind the help that you've given us. Your name needn't come up in any of the investigations into the underhand activities of the Rogers family. I shouldn't need to see you again regarding our department's side of the case.' Detective Bell turned off the recorder.

Sergeant Murray nodded to the constable to take Cliff back to his cell. Bell thanked Murray for his help. He said he now had the knowledge to decide on the best course of action to carry on his investigations. He knew it would take months but he'd get his man, or men in this case, in the end.

Brian Rogers brought a charge of assault against Cliff. Cliff remained silent about the reason he'd assaulted Brian, saying it was a mistake on his part. As Brian's injury was not life threatening, Cliff received a light sentence of six months. When he was released, he moved to a different part of the country, forgetting about Jane.

The Rogers family were investigated thoroughly after surveillance revealed the true nature of night time activities at the boarding house and the social club. Unlicensed gambling and drug activities were rife at the boarding house, although none of the boarders were involved. The Social Club was a front for a brothel. There'd been a suggestion that illegal immigrants were involved but nothing could be proved on that front.

After their trial, the Rogers were imprisoned in separate establishments for fourteen years each.

Running Jump

'Why don't you take a running jump.' His controlling behaviour had to end.

Not used to her disagreeing, he was taken aback for a minute. Laura ran along the cliff path before he could say anything. No longer would she put up with him organising her life.

She felt a hand grip her shoulder. She swung round, handbag outstretched but before she actually hit him, she realised it wasn't Derek.

'The man you ran away from has jumped off the cliff. The emergency services are on their way. He will need to be identified.'

'My brother, Derek. No. No.'

The Punishment

He'd sent the email to the woman arranging where to meet. He'd suggested a walk along the quayside.

Her name was Sally on the dating site. From his brother's photos he knew it was Caroline. He waited for her. No one else was around. When she arrived they started their walk. She looked at him as if she recognised him.

'Do I know you?'

'You knew my brother, Nick.' Before she could run, he pushed her into the water. She screamed, he threw the lifebuoy to her and walked away.

A fitting punishment for contributing to his brother's death.

Bad Friendships

My mother had told us not to associate with that family. I liked Tina and we enjoyed each other's company but her brothers were a bad lot.

We went for a walk along the bank overlooking the train lines, waiting idly to see if my uncle was driving the next train.

Tina's brothers and their gang were walking along the path. When they heard the train, they picked up stones and threw them at the train. We ran away.

Later the police called. A worker had recognised me. I hated giving the names. I was grounded for being there.

The Mysterious Death

Strange, the curtains aren't drawn, Jennifer thought as she approached her employer's house. Mrs Brown usually closed them in the evening when the light faded. This was concerning. Maybe Mrs Brown had risen early for some reason, although she hadn't mentioned yesterday that anything was planned for today.

Jennifer entered the front door, finding it strange again that the alarm wasn't set. Mrs Brown was usually in her bedroom on Jennifer's arrival but if she had risen early, she would've turned it off. Then the third strange thing: the lounge door which was usually kept shut, was ajar.

Jennifer walked towards it, slowly, calling out, 'Mrs. Brown? Are you alright?' There was no answer.

As she pushed the door to open it further, she saw her employer slumped on the sofa - eyes wide open but glazed. It didn't look as if she was breathing.

'Oh, no. Oh Mrs Brown.' Jennifer hurried across and touched the woman's arm. It was cold.

Jennifer reeled back for a second, muttering aloud, 'What should I do? Shouldn't touch her. Not move anything. A magazine on the floor. Who put it there?

Mrs Brown wouldn't be reading it. Oh, dear.' Her hands were moving from her face to her chest. She wanted to reach out to her employer again but stopped herself.

'Ambulance, call the ambulance.' Speaking aloud seemed to help her think straight. She went into the hall, picked up the handset and dialled 999.

The operator soon answered, 'Which service do you require?'

'I don't know. I've just arrived at work. My employer, Mrs. Brown looks … dead.'

'Caller, give me your details in case we get cut off and I can get back to you. What's your name?'

'Jennifer Goode, Mrs Brown's daily help.' Jennifer gave the telephone number and the address. The operator could see the phone number was correct.

'Jennifer, I'll send an ambulance and also inform the police. What room are you phoning from?'

'The phone is in the hall: that's where I am.'

'A police officer might phone you. Stay near the phone and out of the room where Mrs Brown is. The ambulance is on the way.'

'Thank you. I'll do all that. Bye.' Jennifer didn't wait for an answer. She felt shaky, so sat on the stairs, elbows on her knees and face cupped in her hands. She jumped when the phone rang, seconds later.

'Hello, Mrs Brown's home.'

'Hello, is that Jennifer Goode? I'm DC Wendy Long. We've just been informed that you have reported your employer is ill.'

'I've a feeling its worse than that. I only touched her once. Her eyes are open but she's cold.'

'We'll come along straight away. Stay out of the room and don't touch anything. Ok?'

'Yes. Yes, I've got all that. I'll wait here in the hall.'

'Good. We'll be there soon.' As the conversation ended, Jennifer saw her bag in the middle of the hall. She picked it up and took it to the kitchen. That door was open as well. All odd. The doorbell rang.

'Am I glad to see you. Come in,' Jennifer said as she ushered the ambulance staff in.

'You must be Jennifer. I'm Harry and this is my colleague, Cath. Where's Mrs Brown?'

'In the lounge, through that door. I won't go in with you. It's upsetting seeing her like that.'

'I'll go and see Mrs Brown while Cath goes with you to make us all a cup of tea, then Cath can come and help me.' Harry was being solicitous, sensing Jennifer was struggling to stay calm.

'Come on Jennifer, show me the way.' When she filled the kettle, Jennifer noticed a glass in the sink. She hadn't left it there yesterday. Cath was watching her and asked if she could help, noticing Jennifer was shaking.

'I think I'm better kept busy. How do you like your tea? And Harry? I suppose you work together regularly. Funny, that glass wasn't there yesterday when I left. Mrs Brown must've had a drink. I'll wash it with these cups when we're finished.'

Cath gave Jennifer the tea order, then left her to see what Harry was doing. Jennifer busied herself with the task at hand. She wondered about adding biscuits to the tray but decided against it. They weren't really hers to give away. Her hands weren't shaking as much as she concentrated on what she was doing. That glass was a mystery.

The doorbell rang as Jennifer was passing the tray to Cath. A casually dressed couple were standing in the porch.

'I'm DC Wendy Long and this is Detective Sergeant Charlie Smart. You must be Jennifer?'

'Yes, I am. Come in.'

'I see the ambulance has arrived. Which room are the ambulance staff in?'

'The lounge, through that door there.' Jennifer pointed the way.

'Jennifer, would you like to wait in the kitchen? I'll be with you soon and you can help me with a few details.'

'Yes, I'll drink my tea. I need it.' Jennifer walked to the kitchen, still feeling like this was unreal.

Charlie spoke to the paramedics first, after both he and Wendy had put protective clothing on in the hall.

'What are your initial thoughts on Mrs Brown?'

'Definitely deceased when we arrived. Could be a heart attack. She's been dead for some hours.'

'This room's in a bit of disarray. Did Jennifer, Mrs Goode, make a comment about it?'

'Not yet,' Cath said. 'She didn't want to come in here and she didn't say anything when I was in the kitchen with her.'

'Wendy, have a quick look around here and then go and chat with Mrs Goode. If she thinks anything is odd, we'll look into things further. Any relatives been informed?'

'I'm not aware of that. I'll ask Jennifer.' Wendy had a quick look at the magazine, not wanting to touch anything at the moment. She saw that there was a writing pad on the desk. The address had been written at the top right-hand corner with the date below it but nothing else. There were papers scattered on the desk as well. She took her mobile out and took photos of everything to remind herself of the details. Then she went in search of Jennifer.

The sergeant remained to chat with the paramedics.

'Does this look straightforward to you?'

'Well, we're not qualified to judge that, Detective but there's bruising on her arms, as if she's been grabbed by someone. The angle she's sitting at isn't natural. We haven't moved her much, just enough to get her temperature and check for blood pressure, to confirm death. I've taken a photo of how she was when we arrived.'

'Let's have a look. Can you send me that photo, Harry? I think there's a case here for some suspicion. I'll call forensics in.' Charlie gave Harry his mobile number then phoned the forensics team. They would be there in the next few hours.

The door to the kitchen was open so Wendy walked straight in.

'Jennifer, Mrs Brown has definitely passed away, I'm sorry to say.'

'I thought that was the case. Thank you for telling me for definite.'

'How are you feeling?'

'I'm in a right state. Should I phone Mrs Brown's daughter-in-law, Brenda?'

'I'll do that. What family does Mrs Brown have?' Wendy took her notebook out.

'Do you want a cup of tea?'

As Wendy nodded and was opening her notebook, Jennifer carried on talking.

'Her son Steven's in London on business at the moment. His family lives not far from here. Brenda, his wife, pops in on the odd occasion but has a busy social life during school hours. Then Mrs Brown's daughter, Alison and her husband Lionel Handley are on holiday in Florida at the moment with their three children. They live about two hours' drive away, I think, in Somerset. Some way from here in Shropshire so they don't come to visit very often. I have a little notebook in the drawer here with all their contact details, for times of emergency. Ah, here it is.' Jennifer took the notebook out of the drawer and handed it to Wendy, who took a photo of the entries. There were more names further down but they didn't interest Wendy at the moment.

'Jennifer, did you notice anything different this morning to when you left yesterday?'

'Well, first off, I noticed the curtains were drawn back when I arrived. Mrs Brown usually draws them when she goes to bed and I open them when I arrive. Mrs Brown also sets the alarm but that wasn't set. I thought she must've been up early but I've never known her do that. Then the lounge door was open. That was odd as it's kept closed even when Mrs Brown is in. The sight of Mrs Brown, sitting back like that, eyes open and not breathing. Oh, I don't think I shall ever forget that.' She let out a sob and struggled to stop herself crying.

Wendy let her have a few seconds to compose herself.

'Was there anything else?'

'The room's in a mess. The bureau was open, papers everywhere. I can't understand it. Mrs Brown's a tidy person, likes everything in its place. I was tempted to tidy it but then couldn't with her there. Then you said to stay out of the room, so I did. Glad to. The magazine on the floor was not in the house yesterday. Oh and then that glass in the sink. It's bothering me. Mrs Brown doesn't usually drink water, she'd have a cup of tea. The meal I prepared for her is still in the fridge. She didn't eat her supper and she didn't have her usual drink, so who used the glass?'

'Don't touch the glass, Jennifer. I'll take it away with me in a special bag.' Wendy reached into her pocket and brought out an evidence bag. She wrote the details on the outside of the bag then put the glass in and sealed it.

'What time did you leave yesterday?'

'I always leave at the same time, half past two in the afternoon. It gives me time to get to the bus stop for quarter to three. The bus stop's only two houses away but these are all large properties, so it takes a bit of time. Mrs Brown was well when I left, sitting in her living room, reading. She hadn't said that she was expecting any visitors. Yet, when I was standing at the bus stop, I saw a blue car turn into the drive. I didn't recognise it, nor catch a glimpse of the driver.'

'That could be important. Does Mrs Brown leave any washing up for you to do or does she do some herself?'

'Over the weekends she does the washing up, or it would be a mess and she doesn't, sorry, didn't, like the place to be a mess. Maybe she'd leave a cup or plate in the sink but it'd have water in, especially the cup. Then I'd clean that in the morning. Usually, she met friends for lunch on a Saturday and her son and his wife took her out or to their house on a Sunday.'

Jennifer stood up as if to do some washing up at the kitchen sink but Wendy stopped her.

'Don't do any cleaning of any sort, Jennifer. You don't mind me calling you by your Christian name?' Wendy wondered if they were being slightly disrespectful.

'No, I much prefer it.'

'Jennifer, would you mind waiting until the forensics team arrives, so we can take your fingerprints? You see, we don't know if there's anything suspicious about Mrs Brown's death and we want to have as much evidence available to help us make a decision, one way or another. If we have your fingerprints, that will help us to identify if anyone else has been in the house besides you and Mrs Brown. I know it's going to be hard for you to just sit here, waiting and thinking but I'd appreciate it if you could. I'll ask the team to do yours first, then take you home, if that's alright?'

Jennifer became tearful.

'I'll be only too pleased to help. I could catch a bus home, it's every hour.'

'No, I insist on taking you as you've had a very upsetting morning. I'm going to see if there's any news of the forensics team arriving and they won't need any tea or coffee making, so relax if you can. I'll phone Brenda Brown now.'

'She'll most probably be on the school run. Oh, my, it's gone ten o'clock. She'll have dropped them off but she has hands free in her car. You can't tell her that when she's driving.'

'No, I'll ask her to come here as soon as possible. We'll need her to let her family know. If she can't come for some reason, we'll arrange to meet her at her home. I won't be long.'

Wendy left the room with the glass and to phone Brenda away from Jennifer. She also wanted to check up on what was happening in the lounge.

Wendy telephoned Brenda from the porch outside. She asked Brenda to come to her mother-in-law's house as soon as possible. Brenda had nothing on that morning and said she'd be there within half an hour, wondering what the problem could be.

As Wendy entered the lounge, the ambulance staff were just packing up to leave. They'd contacted the pathology technicians to arrange the removal of the body to the morgue for a possible autopsy. They said their farewells and Wendy took the opportunity to update Charlie about her conversation with Jennifer. The two worked well together as a team. Over the past three years they had built up an understanding of what was relevant to their enquiries and he could rely on Wendy to take the initiative when needed, as in this case.

The forensics team arrived and began to set up in the lounge.

'Jenny, could one of your team first take fingerprints from Jennifer, the daily help, please? She's been very helpful but is understandably upset by all of this. We would like to take her home as soon as possible.'

'Sure, Charlie, Tom could do that right away. Are you ready for that, Tom? PC Long will take you to Jennifer Goode.'

Wendy briefly told him about the glass in the kitchen on the way. Tom was gentle with Jennifer, having wet wipes handy to help take some of the dye off her fingers when he had finished. He made a note of Jennifer's details, including her address and date of birth, which Wendy also noted.

Wendy returned to the entrance hall with Jennifer who had collected her belongings ready to go home. They were just about to leave when Brenda, Mrs Brown's daughter-in-law, arrived.

After introductions, Charlie took Brenda to one side and quietly told her what had happened. Brenda was visibly upset as she had a good relationship with her mother-in-law and a great respect for her. Before she and Charlie went into the lounge, Brenda hugged Jennifer and thanked her for being so good about calling the ambulance and the police. Charlie explained that Wendy was taking Jennifer home and would return soon.

On the journey to Jennifer's home, Jennifer's thoughts were in turmoil, while Wendy was thinking ahead about the enquiries which would be undertaken.

'Is anyone at home with you, so you won't be on your own today?'

'My Bob goes to bowls on a Tuesday morning but is usually home around twelve, so he should be in.'

When they arrived at the house, Wendy went in with Jennifer.

Jennifer went straight to him for a hug.

Wendy introduced herself.

'Jennifer found Mrs Brown collapsed this morning. It's been very traumatic for her. She's been a brick in contacting the ambulance and talking to us. She'll need your tender loving care more than usual today,' Wendy explained.

'Jennifer, I'll be in touch in a day or two. Please don't go to the house until we let you know you can. No doubt Steven and Brenda will be in touch with you as well. I'll go back to Mrs Brown's house now.'

'Bye, Wendy and thanks for your kindness.' Jennifer and Bob watched as Wendy drove away.

Charlie was still at the house in Meadow Lane when she returned. Brenda had left as there was nothing she could do at the moment. The forensics team were still examining the property.

'How did Brenda take the news?'

'Shocked at first. I think it took her a few minutes to take in the fact and then to think about everything else related to the death. She said she would be at home if we needed her. She's contacting her husband and Mrs Brown's daughter straight away from home. Is Jennifer alright?'

'Yes, her husband was at home, so she'll tell him her story. They seem a very close couple. Honest and straightforward.'

'Good. I'll go back to the station. Can you stay with this until the body is removed?'

'Yes. Jennifer gave me a spare key in case we should need to return for any reason. I'll sign it in when I return to the station. Shall we organise a patrol to keep an eye on the house during the night?'

'Yes, a good idea. I'll organise that at the station. See you later.'

After Charlie left, Wendy sat in the kitchen keeping out of the forensics team's way. The morgue staff arrived to remove Mrs Brown. That gave the team a chance to get any evidence from the settee where she had lain. Wendy stayed at the house, wandering through the rooms to get a feel for the kind of life Mrs Brown led, while she waited for the forensics team to finish. She noted that Mrs Brown's bed had not been slept in, taking a photo of that for the record. Wendy then returned to the station to type up her notes.

Charlie was in his office early in the morning. He pondered the new case. There was no evidence of foul play. Until the autopsy report arrived, they could not be sure of the cause of death. The bruising on the arms was the only outward clue to another person's involvement at this stage, yet something was niggling Charlie. Why was the room in disarray when the police arrived at the home of Mary Brown?

The detective decided to return to the house and let himself in. Until a cause of death was established, no one, apart from the investigating team, was allowed to enter. After putting on gloves, he looked around the living room. He looked at the photos of the room taken when the body was discovered. Mrs Brown was slumped across the sofa, a magazine on the floor. Her bureau was open and a writing pad was open on the desk. Her address and the date had been written on it and that was all. The chair looked as if it had been pushed to one side.

Forensics had dusted the surfaces for finger marks. They had taken the magazine away for any trace evidence. Charlie walked around the house, not knowing what he was looking for. All the rooms seemed to be in order. In the kitchen, there were only a few cups in the sink. He looked in the fridge. Nothing unusual in there, although some of the food should be destroyed.

He went into the downstairs loo. A spider was swimming in the bowl, so he flushed it. A strange sound came from the cistern. He looked inside and found a small plastic bag containing a piece of paper.

Carefully opening the bag, he found a note. On it was written 'Paul has come again. I can't give him any more money. I fear he will kill me in desperation for his inheritance. If something does happen to me, I do hope someone finds this.'

Just the break Charlie needed. After placing the note into an evidence bag and bagging the outer wet plastic bag separately, he returned to the living room and looked through the bureau for anything with Mrs Brown's handwriting on it. He found her address book and compared the handwriting on the note to some of the entries. To him it looked the same. He called Wendy to tell her about the new evidence.

'Can you contact Jennifer and ask her to come here, possibly picking her up and bringing her? I think we need more information about the family. As she spent more time with Mrs Brown, I'd prefer to hear what she has to say first. We need to know who Paul is.'

'Yes, I'll do that right away and be with you as soon as we can.'

He may have found a reason for a crime being committed but he still didn't know what had caused Mrs Brown's heart attack, if indeed that was the cause of death. He also checked with forensics to make sure they had done a thorough sweep of the whole of downstairs. They said they had gathered finger marks from all the doors, the bureau and all the furniture. They would send their report to him as soon as it was completed.

While waiting for Wendy and Jennifer to arrive, Charlie had a casual look through the drawers in the bureau. He found paperwork was scattered about in there as well. He decided to leave that for Wendy to go through. He was sure that a lot would be revealed from Mrs Brown's bank statements.

Jennifer was mystified when Wendy arrived to collect her to speak to the detective again at Mrs Brown's.

'Hello, Jennifer. Thanks for agreeing to come along so soon. How are you?' Charlie asked.

'Still in shock and strange coming back here. What can I help you with?'

'An item of evidence has come to light. Whose handwriting is in this address book?'

'Both Mr and Mrs Brown used that when he was alive and Mrs Brown continued to use it after his death.' She pointed out those which were Mrs Brown's handwriting.

'Who is Paul?'

Jennifer was taken aback by the question.

'Why do you want to know about him?'

'That name has come up in our investigation.'

'Paul is the illegitimate child of Mr Brown, who had an affair with a local girl. Mr Brown helped finance Paul's upbringing. I thought all that had finished after Mr Brown's death. Besides, Paul has his own business now, which seems to be very successful. He drives around in a big car ....' She paused and looked at Charlie, shocked.

'It could've been his car coming onto the drive. I don't keep up with these things, just sometimes see him around the town. He changes cars a lot.'

'What's the name of his firm?'

'The same as his name, Paul Smith Enterprises. I'm not sure exactly what he does.'

'We can visit him to have a chat. Are there any photos of him here?'

'They were never on show as his existence caused a lot of bother between Mr and Mrs Brown. She didn't want any reminders of Paul but after Mr Brown's death, he came to see her on occasion. I thought he was just taking an interest in her welfare. Mr Brown kept some in the bottom drawer and Mrs Brown never touched them. When I clean the drawers out, I usually put them back where I found them.' Jennifer bent down and opened the bottom drawer of the bureau where she removed an envelope with the photos in.

Charlie took them and spread them over the sofa. Looking at a group photo of four people, Charlie asked Jennifer if she knew who they were.

'I think the older woman is his mother and the man next to her is her husband. The girl is Paul's half-sister and he is standing next to her. She'll be older now.' Charlie tidied the photos away and Jennifer replaced them in the drawer.

'Please don't talk of this conversation to anyone else. We don't want anyone jumping to false conclusions. DC Long will escort you home. However, if you think of anything that could be of help to us, any of Mrs Brown's friends who visited her regularly, will you contact DC Long to let her know, please?'

'I'd be only too pleased to help if I think of something. Poor Mrs Brown.' Jennifer became tearful at the thought of her employer's demise. 'Will you let me know when I can come back to clean things up. It's in an awful mess.'

Charlie said they would keep her informed. The two women left together, DC Long taking Jennifer's arm, as she was quite upset.

Having found the address of Paul Smith Enterprises, Charlie went to the offices which were in a smart block. After introducing himself to the receptionist, he asked to see Mr Smith. Paul came to the desk and took him into his office.

'How can I help you, Detective Smart?'

'It's come to our attention that you were related to the late Mr Brown, the husband of the recently deceased Mrs Brown in Meadow Lane. I wonder if you could explain your relationship with her?'

'That was a shock, finding out about Mrs Brown's death. Brenda phoned to tell me last night. Steven thought I would be interested to know. It seems that you've discovered that I was Mr Brown's illegitimate son. My mother and I were supported by him. She married Sam Thomas when I was six and I have a half-sister. My stepfather and she are good parents. I lived with them until my business took off but now have my own home on the outskirts of town. I can look after myself and a good job too, since no help came after Mr Brown passed away.'

'Did you ever have cause to visit Mrs Brown at her home?' Charlie felt he had to tread very carefully here. Paul was being helpful but his attitude was rather too confident.

'I did on occasion as she was a good old stick and I felt I was keeping an eye on her with her son and daughter not visiting her very often. She always seemed pleased to see me. I think she liked company and with only her cleaner going in the mornings, she must have been lonely.'

'I got the impression that she was a sociable person and had many friends at various clubs and charities she supported.'

Paul looked away when he said, 'Yes, she did but no one seemed to go to the house to see her. It's a bit remote.'

'Thank you for your help. Could I have contact details for you in case we need more information from you? Likewise, if you think of anything that may help us establish exactly what happened the day she died, please could you ring me on this number?' They exchanged business cards.

As Paul showed him to the door, Charlie turned to him and casually said, 'By the way, what car do you drive? Is it that fantastic blue Audi I saw parked at the front of the building?'

Paul smiled. 'Yes, she's a beauty isn't she? Ann, my half-sister, sometimes borrows it, otherwise I don't let anyone touch it.'

'I don't blame you. I trust your sister's an excellent driver.'

'She definitely is or I wouldn't allow her near it.'

Charlie was very thoughtful as he drove back to the police station. Wendy was just packing up for the day when he entered the office. He told her about his meeting with Paul and asked if she knew anything about the family, being local to the town. Wendy said that they seemed to live a quiet life, no problems but she would look at records if he wanted her to do checks on them. Charlie said it could wait till morning.

Charlie thought there had definitely been some kind of harassment that had caused Mrs Brown's heart attack. He decided to do some searches online himself.

He found out that Ann Thomas was a very sociable person and was often seen out at posh restaurants and functions. There was no mention of what she did for a living. Paul himself appeared in lots of society publications but that could be how he ran his business.

He did a quick check for convictions for both of them. Ann had a couple of speeding fines. On the charge cards it stated that she was a model. Paul was once caught for driving over the limit but was not arrested. He was allowed home in a taxi, car impounded for the night, charged and fined with points on his licence.

Looking into the state of Paul's business would be time consuming so Charlie decided to call it a day. He sent an email to Wendy informing her of what he had found out. If she was in before him in the morning, she wouldn't waste time going over the same ground.

The following morning, Charlie was in the office before Wendy. They had a quick debrief when she arrived, along with two detective constables, Dave Green and Mike Phillips, who were involved in the case. Instead of this being a straightforward death, it was becoming more interesting.

The fingerprints had been loaded onto the computer for access by the relevant officers. Dave and Mike searched for possible matches. They were left with three sets of prints which were not identifiable at that stage.

Wendy and Charlie looked into the finances of Paul and Ann. While Paul's company was not in great shape, there were still funds enough to keep it afloat without him panicking into getting money out of Mrs Brown. Ann's were a different story. She had a large overdraft at the bank, three credit cards at their limit and she'd already received letters from bailiffs.

Before confronting the siblings, Charlie decided to speak to Mrs Brown's solicitor, Mr James, regarding her will. They arranged to meet after lunch.

Charlie told Mr James what he'd discovered and wanted to know if there was any provision in Mrs Brown's will for anyone besides her immediate family, as her death was looking more suspicious.

'There's a trust fund for Paul Smith which will mature on the death of Mrs Brown or Paul's fortieth birthday, whichever is the soonest. That's worth five hundred thousand pounds. A smaller trust fund for Ann had also been set up with the same conditions and worth fifty thousand pounds.'

Charlie knew that would definitely clear her debts and leave her with a small balance.

Mr James carried on. 'Jennifer is to receive a lump sum of ten thousand pounds and a small pension for life. Mr Brown had been an astute man in his financial dealings throughout his life. His legitimate children will share the bulk of his estate on the death of his wife.'

The trust fund for Ann was puzzling. Charlie asked the solicitor if he could explain why it was set up.

'It seems her mother had asked him to provide for Ann as well as Paul. Ann's father was a labourer and with Paul being supported by Mr Brown, there was an imbalance in the household. Mr Brown had agreed, out of the kindness of his heart, on condition that there would be no more funding for them from his wife on his death. Mrs Brown was not to know of any of those arrangements. I didn't question why Mr Brown felt he should do this. He was my client and I just followed his instructions.' Mr James hoped that this would be the end of it and that whatever followed would mean that Mrs Brown could be buried peacefully and her children get their rightful inheritance.

When Charlie and Wendy arrived back at the station, they reported all their findings to the Chief, joined by Dave and Mike. The Chief gave permission for them to obtain copies of Ann and Paul's bank statements as well as Mrs Brown's from their respective banks. The detective constables would prioritise analysing the bank statements.

It took twenty-four hours to obtain the bank statements. A pattern of payments emerged, primarily to Ann Thomas. Some to Paul Smith had ceased in the last two years. Charlie and Wendy decided to interview both of them.

Paul was livid at having his accounts searched and protested but realised that was futile. He asked what was being looked for and gave the officers all the details he had of his 'loans' from Mrs Brown. He said there had never been any duress involved in asking for the money. Their agreement was that it would come out of his inheritance and be repaid to Mrs Brown when he reached his fortieth birthday in two years' time.

Ann was a different story. She preferred to be interviewed at the police station. Wendy told her they needed to know the background to her receiving money from Mrs Brown. She shouted and screamed until Charlie and Wendy managed to calm her down. She said it was her right as she had endured endless arguments between her parents when she needed money and couldn't touch Paul's share. She found it hard to get work as a model but sometimes got lucky. She needed to travel a lot on contracts.

'Doesn't your employer pay for your travel?'

'I'm freelance, so have to pay up front then claim it back. They don't always pay up on time. Anyway, what's it to do with you? I didn't kill Mrs Brown. She died of a heart attack.'

'How do you know that?' Charlie asked.

'Well, that's what everyone is saying.'

'Who is everyone?'

'Paul mentioned it. Could've been Brenda who suggested that to him on the phone.'

Charlie decided to drop that point for now. He had another question for her. 'Are you still living at home? I notice that you use your parent's home as your address on your bank statements.'

'I do have a flat but I prefer my mail to go to their house. I'm away a lot and don't want my post in my mail box for days on end.'

'What do you do with your time when you are not modelling?'

'I socialise. I sometimes stay over in other countries if I want to sightsee but not very often. It depends on the money and company.'

'Company? Does that mean your employer, or social contacts?'

'Both.'

It seemed that Charlie wasn't going to get much more out of her.

'Do you have your passport available now?'

'Yes, always carry it on me. Why?'

'I'd like to have a look at it to see where you may have been. Obviously, all EU travel won't be stamped on it but travel further afield will.'

As he turned the pages, Charlie came across trips to the Middle and Far East. Some were more regular than others.

'Is all this travel for modelling jobs?'

'Yes. It's high-end modelling.'

'I am not going to beat about the bush. Are you employed by an escort agency?'

'Yes. There's nothing illegal about that.'

'Not if it is a straight escort agency. Your finances don't reflect a high salary for that kind of work.'

'Sometimes it's just my expenses that are paid and I get a holiday out of it fully paid at the end.'

'Is that all there is to it? No other services required?'

'I don't understand what you are getting at, Detective Smart. Everything I do is above board.'

'When did you last see Mrs Brown?'

'I don't remember. It was probably three weeks ago. I was there with Paul when he paid her a duty visit.'

'What time of day would that be?'

'Usually in the afternoon, so yes, in the afternoon.'

'Did you get on well with her?'

'No, she didn't like me. I don't think she really liked Paul but he was always charming to her. She's rolling in it and could give Paul his inheritance now.'

'Why? Does he need it?'

'No but we could all use extra money from time to time. I bet you could as well.'

Choosing to ignore that, Charlie decided to close the interview for now. He was going to get the detective constables to look into her travelling.

'What was the name of the agency you said you worked for?'

'Dream Team. We help make people live their lives like a dream.' Ann was very serious when she said that. Charlie wanted to laugh and Wendy managed to keep a straight face.

'We need a record of your fingerprints to match them with unidentified marks we found in Mrs Brown's house. Can we deal with that now, while you are here? I'll want to take copies of the pages in your passport as well. It won't take long.' Wendy felt it was time for a break and this would be a good diversion.

'I suppose. Stop me being harassed again by you.'

'We are doing our lawful duty to Mrs Brown. So long as you co-operate, things will run smoother. Can I bring you a drink back with me? Tea, coffee, water?' Ann opted for a coffee. Wendy left the room with Charlie, closing the self-locking door behind them. Charlie organised an officer to take Ann's fingerprints and for the passport to be copied, while Wendy went to the coffee machine for the promised drink. She was wondering if Ann was totally honest about her work.

When she took the coffee back to Ann, she found her speaking on the phone and caught the last part of the conversation.

'… they don't know anything. Ok, I'll be in touch to confirm that job.'

'Sounds promising. Something new lined up?' Wendy was chatty as she gave the coffee to Ann.

'Just a small job down in London. Will I have my passport back today?'

'Yes but we'd prefer you not to leave the country at the moment. Is that going to be a problem?'

'I can't refuse work when it crops up. Nothing's planned at the moment.'

Charlie arrived with the passport and the constable who was taking Ann's fingerprints. When that was done, there was no reason to keep her any longer.

'We'll be in touch should we need to interview you again.'

With that, Wendy escorted her to reception where she watched Ann walk across the car park to a small white Ford Fiesta. No flash car then.

Charlie called Wendy into his office when she returned.

'I have looked at her passport. You have a look at the dates. She's only in the various countries for a day or night at a time. No time for genuine modelling. Time to be an escort but I wonder if there isn't more to her travelling than that. I am going to have a chat with Owen French in narcotics. See if he thinks it's worth pursuing that line of enquiry. Can you check with Dave and Mike on any further developments from the bank statements?'

'Right away. Good luck with Detective French. Hope he's not too busy to see you.'

'We go back a long way, helping each other with investigations when the cases overlap. He is a busy man, you know, which sometimes makes him seem abrupt.'

The detective constables hadn't found anything unusual in Paul's finances. They had been unravelling Ann's with some interest.

'Ann receives money into her account from a company, The Farah Bros, the day before her rent goes out. It is the exact same amount, increasing annually as her rent and service charges rise. There are odd payments from other sources as well but no explanation why. Amounts from Mrs Brown vary, some months nothing at all, others either five hundred pounds or one thousand pounds. Generally, in a year they have totalled five thousand pounds. Wonder if she pays tax on all of this. There are no payments to any accounting firms as far as we can see. Inland Revenue may be interested in this. Ann has a lot going out to a travel agency, Forward Travel, who we found deal mostly in package holidays on a small scale. Possibly she gets discounted travel from them, so worth investigating what she books. We've divided up the enquiries between us, looking into different aspects. Primarily, we're interested in why Mrs Brown has paid her so much money and when it's asked for.' Dave Green had taken on the role of spokesman for the duo.

Wendy was thoughtful. It looked like there was more to Ann's life than just a greedy person.

'Do you have any details of Forward Travel? Managing Director, owner?'

'Yes. All in Colleen Young's name. Here are her contact details.'

'Thanks. Carry on with your enquiries. I'll have a chat with the boss when he's back. I'd like to track Ann's movements, see what she actually gets up to.'

Wendy went back to her desk and created an outline of the case so far. She noted Ann's activities on a second page. Charlie returned from his meeting with Detective French as she finished filling in what they knew. She saved the file in their shared team folder on the server and went to his office.

'How did you get on with narcotics?'

'Very interesting. They've actually been following Ann's movements from a distance as she has associations with persons of interest to them. They don't want us to impinge on their enquiries, so Owen is coming to a meeting with our team in half an hour. What have the others come up with?'

'I've created a file which I've saved in the shared team folder, if you'd like to open it. It's a rough outline of Mrs Brown's case and on page two are the findings from the bank statements, followed by a list of Ann's activities. It's our duty to follow all leads to solve the circumstances of Mrs Brown's death but it's revealed the possible interesting life that Ann leads.'

Wendy paused while Charlie opened the file and studied the facts.

'Yes, much more to this than just a simple case of harassment to obtain money. I'll be interested to get the forensic results on Ann's fingerprints. Ah, Owen has arrived with his constable. Can you gather everyone in here? We should all fit.'

Wendy went out to call the team to Charlie's office, suggesting they bring their chairs with them.

After introductions were made, Charlie explained to the team the reason for narcotics being involved. He asked Dave Green to give a brief on what they had uncovered so far from the bank statements. Owen was impressed by their efficiency and teamwork.

'It looks like you've done a thorough analysis of the bank accounts so far. Some of that information is relevant to our enquiries, particularly the amounts from the Farah Brothers. Is there anything you can add to this DC Long?'

Wendy related the end of the conversation she had heard in the interview room, when Ann said '…they don't know anything.'

'The way Ann was speaking, I took the 'they' to mean us, the police. I pretended I hadn't picked up on that.'

'Nothing definitive in that. I think what we need to do is separate the two lines of enquiry or it's going to get confusing. Having the bank statements is going to help my team enormously. We can track her movements, particularly abroad with our undercover team and match payments coming into her account. Your enquiries should be more simple concerning Mrs Brown's death. Forensics should confirm all your suspicions and enable you to piece together the events. Ours is a more in-depth enquiry which we've been working on for months. Your team have done a great job in unravelling the bank account activities, Charlie. I'd like to suggest at this point that we take over that side of the investigation now.'

'I thought you might say that, Detective French. Pinching my team's thunder. Good job we work for the same side. We'll keep our copy of the statements with transactions relating to Mrs Brown. You can have the rest. Thank you very much for your help in this, Dave and Mike. I'll be with you shortly.' Charlie dismissed the two team members who took their chairs back to the desks where they'd been working.

'Could you spare one of them for a week or two to help my team, as they seem to have got this enquiry under their belts?' Owen was keen to use the knowledge already gained instead of his team wasting time going through it all again.

'Wendy, we can do that, can't we? I'll pass it by the Chief first and let you know.'

'Thanks for your co-operation, Charlie, Wendy.' With that the narcotics duo left. Charlie and Wendy went out to the others who were looking deflated.

'Thanks for your thorough work on those statements, both of you. You're a credit to the team. We do have to carry on with our enquiry regarding payments from Mrs Brown to Ann. However, we have a request for one of you to help narcotics, continuing the analysis of the statements. I have to pass it by the Chief first. Do I have a volunteer?'

Dave Green immediately volunteered. He was eager to finish the job properly and wouldn't be distracted in looking at the background of the payments, except where the narcotics team wanted him to dig deeper. Wendy and Charlie agreed to that.

Charlie stressed to Mike Phillips that the job wasn't finished from their end yet and they needed the detail of all transactions involving Mrs Brown including the total of the transfers for their case.

The Chief agreed to one of Charlie's team helping the narcotics team on a temporary basis.

The following day, the results of the fingerprint matches were back. The magazines on the floor had finger marks which matched to Ann's fingerprints. Matches were also found on the bureau where Mrs Brown had been writing, on some of the papers scattered around and the glass found in the kitchen. Ann had definitely been in the house the day of Mrs Brown's death.

The Chief Inspector gave permission for Ann to be brought in for another interview. Wendy tried to contact her by landline, then by mobile phone. When Ann eventually answered, the line was crackling. Wendy managed to ascertain that Ann had flown to Islamabad that morning and was due to return in two days' time. Wendy said she would contact Ann on her return. The interview would have to wait but they could gather more details of the case in the meantime.

Charlie advised Wendy to take some time owing, while they couldn't move the case further on and nothing else was urgent. She was pleased about that as her fiancé was on leave for the week. They could do with quality time together.

Wendy spent the rest of the day tidying up the background paperwork for the case. As they had all the evidence they needed now, Wendy was pleased to be able to tell Steven that their enquiries were at an advanced stage now and they wouldn't need to return to his mother's house. Steven said he would collect the key from the reception desk at the police station when he was next passing. He mentioned that Brenda had been keeping in touch with Jennifer. They were all coming to terms with the fact of Mrs Brown's death and her funeral arrangements were in hand.

Wendy guessed that Jennifer would be pleased she could 'tidy up' Mrs Brown's home and hopefully Steven would tidy up his mother's paperwork.

On her return to work two days later, Charlie brought Wendy up to date on the latest developments. Narcotics had latched on to Ann's disappearance. Their undercover officer had followed her to Islamabad and checked into the same hotel. He had proof of whom she was meeting with. He also followed her when she left the hotel except into the building of Farah Bros. When she left the building, she was carrying a small parcel, neatly gift-wrapped.

Ann had dinner in the hotel that night, with another couple and a man of middle Eastern origin. That seemed above board. She went to her room alone. She was on her way back to the UK, flight due to land in Manchester at midday, so was expected to arrive at her flat in Shrewsbury around three o'clock in the afternoon. Another undercover narcotics officer was going to follow her from the airport. Customs wouldn't be searching her, on instructions from narcotics, as they wanted to see if the parcel was to be delivered to anyone else. They did not know its contents.

'Are we allowed to interview her today, as planned? I could telephone her around three to arrange for her to come in to see us.' Wendy wanted their case solved, yet the other team had a more urgent priority.

'Yes, we may interview her,' Charlie said. 'We can establish why she had been to see Mrs Brown. We can also ask her relevant questions regarding the glass, the magazines and the papers on the desk. We are requested not to arrest her as narcotics want her to be trapped if she's a drugs mule.'

'Understood. It's no fun working with our hands tied behind our backs. At least we don't have to get a solicitor involved on her behalf at this stage.'

'Yes, that will come later if narcotics can nail her. Otherwise, our case will take priority to get it wound up and they can go after her in their own sweet time.' Charlie also didn't like to have cases left hanging in the air when they could be closed.

At three o'clock, Wendy telephoned Ann. She answered immediately. She had just arrived home and was unpacking.

'Could you come to the station in the next hour as we have a few details we would like to discuss with you?' Wendy kept a friendly tone to her voice although she wanted to be more demanding.

'I have someone to meet in half an hour but I could be with you around four thirty. Would that be too late for your home time?'

'That would be fine. I'll expect you then.'

Wendy wondered if Ann was still being followed. She just hoped she could wind up her case before narcotics became over-zealous.

Ann arrived at the front desk at the appointed time. At least she could be relied on for that, thought Wendy.

In the interview room, Wendy asked if she could record their discussion, so she wouldn't have to make notes. Ann was puzzled by this as she saw that Wendy already had a file in front of her but she agreed.

'Ann, we have the results of all the forensic examinations regarding the death of Mrs Brown. We've found your fingerprints match those taken in various places in the house.'

'Well, I had been there some weeks before Mrs Brown passed away.'

'We believe these are more recent than that. They were on the magazine found on the floor, on the papers scattered on the bureau, on a glass in the kitchen sink and on cupboard doors in the kitchen. Any comment?'

Ann realised she couldn't protest any more. She broke down and told her story.

'I'd been to see Mrs Brown to borrow money from her. I always told her it was Paul who requested it to help his business. I told Mrs Brown he felt embarrassed about asking for the money as the family had helped him all his life.

'Mrs Brown refused to help me this time. I lost my temper. In a panic I pushed Mrs Brown out of the way and rummaged through her desk where she had been about to write a letter. Mrs Brown had stumbled across to her sofa to get away from me. I grabbed her arms, shouting at her to write a cheque for me. Mrs Brown had taken a breath as if to say something, then suddenly slumped back on to the sofa.'

'I didn't know what to do. It was a shock seeing her face like that, eyes staring at me. I couldn't call the ambulance. I shouldn't have been there. I couldn't breathe properly. I went to the kitchen and searched the cupboards for a glass and drank some water. I ran out of the house, the door locking on its own behind me. I had to steady myself in the car to drive it back to Paul's office. I have my own keys and left in a taxi to go home. I didn't think that she was dead. Never seen a dead body before. Paul told me about it two days later. What's going to happen now?'

Wendy looked at her with pity. 'Had you called an ambulance, the woman might have been saved.' Ann made no comment.

'I want to tie up some loose ends. Did you take the magazine to Mrs Brown for a reason?'

'No, I had bought it to read. I don't know why I took it into the house with me, just habit of not leaving my belongings in Paul's car.'

'Why did you need the money?'

'I haven't had a lot of work lately. The agency expect me to go to my assignments looking like a thousand dollars but don't want to pay me the expenses I need. As I am to inherit on Mrs Brown's death, I thought I could have some in advance. I don't know why she didn't want to play ball this time.'

'We notice that you have money coming from Farah Bros into your bank account which then appears to pay your rent. Can you explain that?'

'Mr Farah was my mother's employer. She cleaned in the offices and he took a liking to her. They are still kind of friends. When he found out I was still living at home, he offered to pay my rent so Mum and Dad could have their house to themselves. It's good to be away from there as my Dad can be really obnoxious at times. I think he's always been jealous of Paul's parentage. Mr Farah likes me to visit

211

him from time to time and gives me gifts to bring back for my Mum.'

Wendy contained her excitement at these revelations in case she was barking up the wrong tree.

'Thank you for your honesty, Ann. For now, I'll complete my notes on this case and discuss with my senior officer where we go from here. I'll let you know soon. I wonder, do you have your passport with you? I think we should keep that here for now, if you don't mind.'

'Well, I do mind. I should be going on an assignment in Dubai next week.'

'I can't promise you'll have it back by then. You may miss that opportunity. I'll be in touch soon.'

At the front desk, Wendy gave Ann a receipt for the passport. Ann looked perplexed as she left.

Mike Phillips had spent some time during the past two days looking into Ann's travel bookings. He discovered that the Farah Bros also paid some of Ann's travel expenses, contrary to what she had told them. They had a big hold on her.

Wendy saw that Charlie was free and asked if she and Mike could go in to discuss the case.

'I think you will be interested in this recording, Charlie and Mike.'

Wendy played it to them and they were thinking along the same lines as Wendy.

'Have you heard from narcotics lately, Charlie? I think they know about this already.'

'No, I haven't. I'll talk to the Chief and see what he has to say. As for Ann, I think we should discuss with the CPS what she should be charged with. A pity Mrs Brown took so long to stand up to her, especially with her weak heart. It was a good move, keeping Ann's passport for secure reasons. She can most probably have it back soon.'

Wendy and Mike returned to their desks to write up their notes while Charlie had his talk with the chief.

Before they left for the day, another meeting was called in the Chief Inspector's office. When Wendy and Mike arrived, they were not surprised to see Detective French and his team there.

'We can now conclude two investigations which have strangely overlapped to everyone's benefit.' Chief Inspector Jeremy Collins was puffed up with pride, knowing that his team was instrumental in helping narcotics, for a change.

'Do you want to explain, Detective French?'

'Thank you, Chief. As you all know, we have been following Ann Thomas closely for several months, as she's associated with the Farah family. We didn't know how deeply involved she was until your team requested her bank statements. She regularly visits them in Islamabad and also, as it happens, in their offices in Dubai. We've not been able to tell if she is a drug mule, until today. We followed her from the airport to her flat, then to her mother's home and on to here. We noticed that she carried a large bag with her to her mother's home and left it there. At this point, our officers are searching her parents' property for the bag and its contents.' He waited for that to sink in, then continued.

'We've also managed to obtain access to the Thomas' bank accounts. They spend more money on their lifestyle than what goes into their bank accounts. We've followed Mr Thomas closely. He passes on packages to a lot of shady characters. An undercover colleague intercepted one containing heroin and cocaine. We didn't know for sure where they came from. Your questioning of Ann helped us. She's either very clever or very naïve. No doubt, if our suspicions are proved, we'll find out everyone's involvement. Why she had to extort money from Mrs Brown when her parents could have supported her, goodness knows.'

'Thank you, Detective. Until we know the outcome of the raid which is taking place now, we shall not know how we'll be proceeding with the case against Ann, which we must complete. However, if she's oblivious to the contents of the packages she gives to her parents, she could become a witness for the prosecution. Tomorrow we'll know more. Thank you everyone, for your efforts.'

The meeting broke up. It felt like an anti-climax. Wendy hoped that the following day would bring more conclusive evidence.

And it did.

The packages did contain cocaine and heroin. Sam Thomas had a deal going with the Farah brothers. They paid Ann's expenses. Her father kept fifty percent of the drug takings. Ann took that money in a package back to the Farah brothers.

Sam didn't trust his wife. He had married her out of pity. He controlled everything she spent and dictated what holidays they took. Ann felt forced into doing what her father told her to do, to protect her mother. She couldn't see a way out of it. They were both victims of

215

domestic abuse. Paul Smith had no idea how bad things were with his mother and half-sister, as he'd left home as soon as he could. Ann didn't tell him the truth when they met as she saw no way he could intervene.

The inquest into Mrs Brown's death, following an autopsy, concluded that she died of a heart attack, brought on by the assault by Ann Thomas and her reckless behaviour in not calling for help. The CPS decided there was not enough evidence for a court case against her as Mrs Brown had an underlying heart condition. Ann had agreed to be a witness for the prosecution which went in her favour as well.

However, the family threatened to bring a civil case against Ann which was dropped when she agreed to give up her inheritance from Mrs Brown.

Sam Thomas was charged with the illegal dealing of drugs. He was also charged with abusive behaviour towards his wife and daughter. They brought charges against him when they were arrested. He was imprisoned for sixteen years for drug dealing and money laundering and a further ten years for the abuse of his wife and daughter

Lucy Thomas was not charged as it was proved she was a victim in this case, too weak to stand up to people stronger than her and her evidence was vital.

Although Ann was charged with being a drug mule, that sentence was suspended, pending no further criminal activity.

The Brown family were relieved when the inquest was over, as they could bury their mother and at last put closure to their association with the Thomas family and Paul Smith.

Lucy and Ann Thomas stayed in the area for several months while the suspended sentence was filled. Then they moved abroad. Lucy had divorced her controlling husband. Paul visited them regularly in their mansion on the Costa del Sol. At least some good came out of Sam stashing away some of the ill-gotten gains, found in a rusty old suitcase in the garage rafters when the roof collapsed after a storm. They were fortunate that the notes were still legal tender.

Printed in Great Britain
by Amazon

57479708R00129